DRITA
My Homegirl

DRITA

My Homegirl

by JENNY LOMBARD

SCHOLASTIC INC.

New York Toronto London Auckland Sydney
Mexico City New Delhi Hong Kong Buenos Aires

ISBN-13: 978-0-439-02006-0
ISBN-10: 0-439-02006-9

12 11 10 9 8 7 6 5 4   8 9 10 11 12/0

Printed in the U.S.A.   40

First Scholastic printing, January 2007

Design by Marikka Tamura

Text set in Dante and Goudy Sans Medium

For my students

ACKNOWLEDGMENTS:

The story of Drita and Maxie has been coming together
for a long time and many different people helped me along
the way. I would like to thank:

• The children I've worked with for teaching me so much about
friendship, family and life.
• The Wurlitzer Foundation of Taos, New Mexico,
for providing a quiet place to work.
• Henry and Wendy Owen-Dunow
for recognizing the writer inside the first-grade teacher.
• Jennifer Carlson of the Dunow Carlson Agency
for her editorial insights and her unwavering support.
Without her vision, this book would never have happened.
• Susan Kim for her dramaturgical insight.
• Kirk Lombard for the tough love and the basketball expertise.
• Samantha Nelson for helping me understand
what kids sometimes feel.
• Persiana Cota for her linguistic and cultural knowledge.
• John Rudolph, Nancy Paulsen and the editorial staff at Putnam
for their commitment to this project.
• Julian Marshall for inspiration.
• Scott Marshall for foot rubs, spaghetti sauce
and everything in between.

DRITA

My Homegirl

1

DRITA

FOR THREE DAYS, before I am coming to this country, I can't eat. My mother is afraid I'm sick, and the Americans will turn us away when we get to New York City, but my grandmother said don't worry: now that my father has his American job, no one can turn us away. She said it's just the excitement taking away my appetite. For once my *gjyshe* is wrong about something: It's not excitement that keeps me from eating my dinner, it's worry. I keep wondering: What if I don't know my own *baba* when I see him at the airport? It's been almost one year since we are together with my father. The more I think about it, the more worried I get.

Finally, on the day we are leaving for New York, I get so tired of worrying, I eat a big bowl of delicious *trahana* my grandmother makes for me. While I eat, I think to myself: this is the last food I will taste in my country.

Our plane lands in New York in the middle of the night. At the airport, I can feel how hot New York is compared to the Balkans. Even the air feels different on my skin, sticky and wet. I close my eyes for a minute and take a breath. I think to myself, Now I am breathing American air.

Even though it's the middle of the night, this place is crowded with people. Then I see him: his face is all furry with a red beard he is growing, and he looks thinner, but he is still wearing his Albanian clothes. Now I know it was silly to worry so much. Of course I know my own father.

"Mirë se erdhët," my father shouts, welcoming us, and sweeps my mother and my baby brother up into his arms. My mother is crying and we are kissing him so much. My mother cried every day that we were in Kosova because we had to be separated from Baba for so long. For one year my father was alone in America, getting money for us to come here. Maybe now that we are together in New York City, she will stop her crying.

My father kisses me on top of my head, and we follow him through the airport to the garage where he parked his taxicab. When we learned that my father's first American job was as a car driver, we were all sad that a man who had trained as an electrical engineer had to take a job that was *s'ësh të në dinjitetin e tij*—not good enough for him. But when I saw my father's taxicab, I thought it was lucky my father's first American job was as a driver. Now we would have a pretty yellow cab to take us to our new home, just like in a movie.

I look over at my grandmother. Gjyshe hasn't said a word since we got off the plane, except to nod hello to her son. Now she looks at me and smiles a smile so big that it covers her whole face.

"America the beautiful!" she says in English.

Sometimes from the way she smiles and tells jokes, my *gjyshe* seems more like a girl eight years old than an old lady almost seventy.

My father opens the trunk and puts our bags inside while the rest of us pile into the car. My grandmother, brother and I are in the backseat and my mother is in front.

"*Zonjë!*" says my father and makes a little bow. Inside, the car smells sweet, like perfume. Gjyshe and I watch silently as my father drives the car down the ramps and tunnels of the airport. Soon we are on the streets, with the lights of America everywhere around us.

How does my father know where we were going? He must have learned enough about America to fill a book. Does he have any American friends? While I think these things, my mother talks, talks, talks in the front seat, telling how it has been for us in the ten days since we left Prishtina: the crowded bus we rode when we left the city, the soldiers with their guns, the Albanian people we met living in tents by the side of the road, and finally the airport, where a man checked our visas and made her cry.

My father just nods and keeps his eyes on his driving, and the dark and twisting streets of New York City move past us like a blur. Just looking makes me tired. I wish to see where Baba is taking us, but soon I am falling asleep.

When I open my eyes again, it is morning. Now I have a new home and a new country, I think to myself. But as I look around, I begin to feel sad.

My new American home is just an *apartament*, smaller even than our house in Prishtina. And everywhere you look in this new American house, there is something dirty and old: walls that have the dirt from cooking on them, a ceiling that has pieces of paint falling down, windows that have so much gray dirt, you can't see from them. Even outside the glass there is nothing to see except an old dirty wall.

At breakfast, no one is talking about our dirty new American house, but you can tell we are all thinking the same thing from the way my mother brushes off the chair before she sits down and Gjyshe stirs the *trahana* like she believes something is going to jump out of the pot. Even my baby brother sniffs his bowl before he takes a bite of his breakfast. My father looks at his family and puts down his coffee cup.

"Zot! What could I do?" he says in Albanian. "This was

the only place we could afford! We are lucky to have it—and this furniture too! Look at this table and chairs! All of it was a gift!"

"All of it dirty, a gift for the poor," my mother says with a sound like crying coming up in her voice.

"Please, my wife! Let us enjoy our first American breakfast together." But it is too late. My mother rushes from the table and into her little room, slamming the door behind her.

"Dashi!" my father says, calling her by her first name. Now he is up from the table too.

Through the closed door, I can hear my mother crying. I hear my father too, speaking to her in a quiet voice, trying to calm her. But it won't help. I know why my mother is so sad.

"Grandmother, is Cousin Zana *e zhdukur*?"

My grandmother puts her arms around me. "Sshh, Drita. Not now."

Even worse than those who were forced to leave their homes, like my family, are the people who are *zhdukur*— disappeared. Because I am a child, I am not supposed to know about the *zhdukur* like my mother's favorite cousin Zana. But of course I do. Everyone does.

"Come. In a few days, you will start your new school, but right now I need your help."

My grandmother takes a big bucket and a yellow brush from under the sink.

"Wah! Wah!" my brother yells as she fills the bucket with

soapy water. Soon we are on our knees, cleaning the floor with a yellow brush. My brother helps too, stirring the water with his fat little hand.

"*Sillet Bota anembanë, njerëzia lenë vatane, dhe po shkojmë në kurbet . . .*" my grandmother sings.

At first it feels strange, listening to this old Albanian song in a dirty new American kitchen. But soon I begin to sing myself.

"*Të vendosim ardhmërinë, se e humbmë dashurinë, do të humbim dhe fëminë . . .*"

My grandmother is a very wise woman, I think. She knows that when you are sad and far away from home, the best thing to do is to sing a song in your strongest voice.

I wish my mother knew that too.

2

Maxie

IF YOU ASK ME, the most unlucky, annoying day of the week has got to be Monday. Spelling quizzes, bad hair days, bologna sandwiches for lunch—it seems like the worst stuff gets saved up for Mondays. "Stormy Monday" is what my grandma always calls it. She's even got a little song she sings around the house all about it.

> *"Oh, it's Stormy Monday, I'm feeling oh so sad,*
> *Lord, it's Stormy Monday, I'm feeling oh so sad,*
> *Blues are raining down on me, and I'm feelin' oh so*
> *mad . . . "*

When I was seven, I thought that song was just about a rainy day that happened to be on Monday. But now that I'm a fourth grader, I know exactly what that song means. It means Mondays are bad news.

Today is no different. When I get up, my daddy is there, reading the paper while my grandmother makes some eggs. Usually my dad is gone by the time I get up, but not today.

"Good morning, Maxie," my dad says real cheerful and puts down his paper. I think to myself, Uh-oh, now what is this? My grandmother is in the kitchen acting all busy over at the sink, but I can tell she is hanging on every word.

"Okay, what did I do this time?" I say, and I'm wondering if he looked in his pipe box yet and found out I broke his big fruitwood pipe. It really was an accident, I was just playing.

"Haw haw," Daddy says, rubbing on my head. "You didn't do anything, my smart girl. Can't a daddy talk to his only daughter?"

Now I know it's something really bad.

"Maxie. I have a friend I want you to meet," he says.

"Who, you mean like Uncle Herbie?" I say, thinking maybe I'm going to go bowling again. My uncle Herbie is my dad's oldest friend. He's got a purple bowling ball with his initials on it and has a doorbell at his house that can play a whole song.

My daddy coughs like he's got a piece of toast stuck in his throat. "No, Maxie, not Uncle Herbie. A woman friend."

"Oh," I say, and I look down at my eggs.

"Her name is Lisa. She works at the bank with me. I think you'll like her, honey. She even has a little boy, four years old."

I push my egg over to the side, looking for white stuff. Sometimes when my grandma makes scrambled eggs she doesn't cook them all the way through, which I hate.

"Baby girl, aren't you going to say something?" Daddy asks.

"Grandma, you didn't cook these eggs enough," I say.

"Answer your father," my grandma says.

"Congratulations, Daddy," I say, reaching for my juice, "can't wait to meet her. I'm sure she's a reeeeeeeeal fine person."

My daddy shoots Grandma a look, and no one says anything else about no Lisa after that, which is just fine with me.

"Go on and get dressed, Maxie," Grandma says. "And no dawdling this morning. I don't want to be late."

"Dawdling" is what my grandma calls it when you're late going different places like school and piano lessons. In my family, I got the reputation for dawdling. My grandma says it happens when I'm upset about something, but that's not true. I just like to take my time doing things, like getting dressed in the morning.

Inside my room, I open my top drawer to look for some socks, but it's empty because my grandma didn't do the laundry yet this week. Then I spy one of my new rainbow toe socks my daddy just bought me lying under my bookshelf. I really like those toe socks.

Outside the door, Grandma and Daddy are talking.

"Gerald, she needs more time . . ." goes my grandma.

"How much time does she need? It's been three years already," my daddy says back.

"Three years is nothing for a child," Grandma says.

Blah blah blah. Blah blah blah. It seems like my grandmother and my daddy are always fighting about me lately. Usually, my daddy is saying I've got to be more grown-up and my grandma is saying no way—I don't because of what happened when I was seven. Sometimes I agree with my daddy, sometimes I agree with Grandma, but most of the time I think they both got a point.

I start looking around for my other toe sock, but I can't find it anywhere.

"She needs to think of something besides herself once in a while—and I don't mean that damn hamster!" my daddy says.

"Gerald! Language!" goes my grandma because you're not supposed to use curses in my house, even little ones.

Over by the window, there's Cupcake, waving at me from her Habitrail. Cupcake is my dwarf hamster. I named her that because she's so white and fluffy that she looks good enough to eat. Ever since Cupcake escaped and hid under the radiator, I don't think my daddy likes her too much.

"Want to go in your exercise ball?" I ask her. Cupcake sticks her nose out of her nest and sniffs at me. In hamster language, that's definitely a "Yes!"

Real careful, I lift the top of her cage and take her out.

"Squeak!" says Cupcake.

I put her on my shoulder, because I'm trying to train her to ride around up there. The only thing is, she doesn't really like that too much. She decides to run down my back.

"Hey!" I say, and I lean over so she doesn't fall off and hurt herself.

"Where are you going?" I ask her, because now she's running down my leg and onto the floor. She just wrinkles her nose and laughs at me. Then she goes right under the bed.

"Wait," I go and I dive after her.

Wow, there's a lot of stuff under here! I think to myself because now I've found about twelve things I've been looking for, including my light-up pen, last week's science homework, and half a candy bar. I guess that's why my grandma is always after me to vacuum under the bed when I clean my room. Then way at the back, almost to the wall, I see Cupcake sitting on my other toe sock. Real slow, I grab one end of the sock and start to pull her out.

"Are you hurrying?" my grandma yells through the door, just as I grab Cupcake off the sock.

"Poor thing!" I say, holding Cupcake against my chest.

Her heart is beating so fast, she must have been scared by her toe-sock ride. I lie back down on the bed, give her a chance to nestle. Just for a second I close my eyes.

The minute I do, this bad feeling comes over me. Then it's like my brain is a broken record. "LISA! LISA! LISA!" goes my head.

That's when my grandma comes charging into the room, my daddy right behind her.

"Squeeeeeeeeeak!" Cupcake says and jumps off the bed.

"Oh no, not again!" hollers my daddy, scooping her up off the floor.

"Get up this minute!" yells Grandma, throwing back the covers.

Before I know it, Cupcake is back in her cage, I'm wearing rainbow toe socks and my least favorite dress and I'm hauling out the door on the way to school.

"It's time for school!" they yell.

What would my family do without me? If it weren't for me, there wouldn't be anything they agree on.

3

DRITA

"Hurry, Drita!" says my father. "We don't want to be late!"

I jump into the front seat of the cab. After too many days of cleaning and other chores, today I am finally going to my new school, PS 18 of Brooklyn.

On the street, a lady with a yellow scarf on her head pushes her baby in a *karrocë*; a boy flies by on a silver *motorçikletë*. We pass a bazaar and I see so many stores, all selling different things: some waving colorful shirts and dresses from their windows like flags, others growing buckets of brooms and mops, still others with *fruta dhe perime*—fruits and vegetables piled in mountains. It seems strange to me that just two days ago, when my father took me to this market, I thought it was wrong to stare. But now after three days in this country I know the opposite is true: in America, there are so many colors, you must look at everything twice.

"Look out! American girl going to school!" my father jokes and gives the horn a push.

I am so happy, I kick my feet against the front of the cab. My new American sneakers light up.

My father is right. Even before we come to this country, everyone says I am already like an American girl. That's because I love everything about America—American films, American TV, even American sports—basketball is my favorite. And this was my special surprise when I woke up today: my father gives me a gift of some new basketball shoes with lights on the bottom. Now I can be like the other students, wearing stylish clothing and playing sports every day.

My father drives and drives around the streets. Finally he stops in front of a tall building.

"Look, Drita," my father says, "your new school."

When I imagine my school, in my head I am always seeing a place like on my favorite TV show, *Saved by the Bell*. But my school does not have red bricks and a white roof like Bayside High. Instead it is plain gray with a park in front. My father stops the car and we get out. Then we hear a voice calling.

"Hello! Adem!" says a voice. I see a woman hurrying to meet us. She is older than Nënë but younger than my *gjyshe*. She has a round, plain face and she is wearing a flowered dress.

"My friend," says my father, holding out his hand. "Miss

Mirfue, this is my daughter Drita. Drita, this is Miss Mirfue. She works for the human rights organization that helped us leave Kosova. She is going to help you too, by going to the new school and filling out forms."

"How are you?" Miss Mirfue says in Albanian.

"I am well!" I say back, trying not to laugh. It is so strange to me to notice that she speaks our language with an American accent!

"Are you ready for your first day, Drita?" she says.

"Oh, Miss Mirfue, Drita has been ready since she was born!" My father laughs, but then he gets back into his taxicab.

"Wait, Baba! Aren't you coming?" I ask him.

"Drita, I must return the cab to the garage," he says. "I drove all night and if I don't get back to the garage by nine o'clock, they charge me more."

"You mean, I have to go all alone?" I ask him. I don't mean to show my father I am afraid, but I can't help myself. Now instead of feeling happy about going to a new school, for one moment I think I might cry.

"You won't be alone. Miss Mirfue is coming with you," he says.

"Come, Drita," Miss Mirfue says. "You can take my hand if you want."

My father looks at me. In his face is a question. Are you a grown-up girl, or a baby like Hashim? he seems to ask.

15

"Well?" asks Miss Mirfue, waiting.

"No, thank you," I say. "I am already ten years old."

My father hugs me tight.

"Your mother will pick you up from school. Have a good day, *zemra ime*," he says. My sweetheart.

Miss Mirfue and I walk up the stairs to the school. Inside the building, a lady police officer points to a doorway and we go inside to the school office. Miss Mirfue talks to a lady with red hair and a long gold chain around her neck. All around the room, people are coming are going and there is lots of noise from a copying machine and many telephones. Then someone says my name. A large man is walking over to us. He smiles at me and shakes my hand. His face is friendly.

"Drita," Miss Mirfue says in Albanian. "This is Mr. Littman. He is the principal of the school. He will take you to your new class."

I am so excited when I hear these words that my heart starts banging inside me like a drum. I walk with Mr. Littman down a long hallway with voices and footsteps echoing everywhere. Then we stop at a door. A young pretty woman is standing there. I know just who she is.

"*Miss Salvato*," my teacher says, pointing to herself.

I will tell you what is strange for an Albanian person like me in an American school. It is not the largeness of my school, bigger even than the National Library in Prishtina. It is not the classrooms, with children's stories and pictures and artwork everywhere. It is not even my new teacher, who is young and pretty, instead of old and grumpy like Mr. Shabani at home.

In Albania, there is a wall. On one side are the Serbian children and their teacher, also a Serb. On the other side, that is where we Muslim children sit, with Mr. Shabani our teacher. When we learn to read, we have separate books. When we sing, we know different songs. We speak our language, not theirs. We even use separate toilets when we have to go to the bathroom.

When I first step into my American classroom, I see all the faces here have different skin and different eyes and different hair from each other, but they are all sitting in one room, with no wall. And they are all looking at me.

Miss Salvato says something to them and I hear my name. I know she is telling them who I am. I say the words in English just like my father teaches me.

"My name is Drita Kelmendi," I say. "I am here."

But in my head, I speak in my language too.

"Quhem Drita Kelmendi. Jam këtu."

4

Maxie

"You in trouuuuuuuuuuble!" says my friend Brandee as soon as I walk into my classroom.

"Shut up, Brandee," I say out of the side of my mouth. Leave it to her to let the whole world know I'm late, just when I'm about to sneak into the classroom nice and quiet.

My teacher jumps up. "Good morning, Maxie! I'd like to see your note, please," says Miss Salvato.

"Uh, I don't have a note, Miss Salvato," I say.

"Why not?" she asks. Unfortunately my teacher is really strict about stuff like that.

"Well, my grandma said we were so late, she didn't have the time to write one," I say, and the whole class giggles.

"In that case, I'm going to have to mark you tardy, Maxie. You know what that means," says Miss S. Of course I do.

Five "tardies" and you get study hall. Who could forget about that?

But I'm not worrying about that because now I notice something weird.

"Who's that?" I ask because someone is sitting at my desk.

"Oh, Maxie," Miss S. says, "I need to ask you a favor. . . . We have a new student in our class. There was no place for her to sit when she arrived this morning and you were the only person who wasn't here. Would you be so kind as to share a desk with Brandee until the custodian brings another desk upstairs for her?"

Didn't I tell you Monday is my worst day?

I look over at the new girl who's sitting at my desk. I got to say, I don't like her. I don't like her hair, I don't like her clothes, I don't like her face and I don't like her eyes. She's the kind of white person who's so pale, she's like a ghost—you think you can see right through her.

"She look like Heidi," Brandee whispers in my ear.

Just in case you don't know, *Heidi* is this movie about a girl and her grandfather. We all know about her because they always show that movie in the auditorium when it's raining outside. It's so old and played out that it's got no color, just black and white. Brandee was right, this new girl does have her hair in two long braids just like Heidi.

19

"Maxie, I'd like to introduce you to your new classmate. This is Drita Kelmendi."

"Drita. What kind of name is that?" Brandee says, reading my mind.

"Sounds like something you use to clean out a drain—Drita Draino," I say, just to make her giggle.

Okay. I got to tell you a few things about myself. First off, Miss Salvato is my favorite teacher ever and I don't usually give her a hard time. Second, someday I want to be a big comedian and performer. Sometimes, I have this problem of treating school like my own private comedy show, where it's my job to make people laugh, which is why my teachers told my father and Grandma that I can be "challenging" in school. If I stop being challenging, my dad is going to take me on a trip to Six Flags. But it's kind of hard to remember that when you get on a roll.

"Maxie, I'd like to talk to you privately when the rest of the class is at recess," my teacher says. That means I have to wait for five minutes by the gate while she dismisses the class. When she comes back over, I figure she's going to yell at me about having an attitude—but, as usual, my teacher really surprises me.

"Maxie, I owe you an apology," she says finally. "I shouldn't have allowed another student to sit at your desk without asking you first. I can understand how that would upset you."

"Thank you, Miss Salvato," I say, and I feel lucky to have a teacher who's pretty and nice too.

"*But . . .* " she says. Somehow I just knew there was going to be a "but."

"You weren't very welcoming to our new student. Frankly, I was a little surprised. Is something bothering you today?"

I open my mouth to tell my teacher about something named Lisa, but then I shut it again.

"Not really."

Miss Salvato looks at me like she's thinking about something.

"I wonder, did you pick a social studies theme to research yet?"

"I still can't make up my mind about that," I say.

"I think you should pick Drita."

"Say what?" I say because my teacher does have some crazy ideas sometimes.

"Drita comes from Kosovo. Her home has been in the news a lot lately. The story of how she came to our school is very unusual. I was going to tell the class about her myself, but now I think you should do it."

"Well, what is her story, then?"

"You're going to have to find out."

"But she doesn't speak any English!" I say.

"Then it will be a wonderful challenge for you," Miss Salvato says and smiles at me, just as sweet as can be.

"You're free to go now. Have a wonderful recess," she says.

Outside, my peeps got their rope going for double Dutch. Tasha, Brandee, Kayla, Evaliz—all my friends are there.

"Crocodiliosus goes quack quack quack—hit it! Señorita, your momma smells like pizza. Señora, Señora, forgot to shut the doora . . ." they're singing.

"Maxie, jump in!" Tasha yells.

I look over my shoulder to where Miss Salvato is watching me, arms folded, over at the door.

"Not right now, Tash," I say.

The new girl with the funny name is standing by the bench. Right away, I notice her sneakers are new and pretty fly. It makes me wonder if she went shopping with her mom just to get ready for her first day at school. That used to be the best thing about starting school.

"So, where do you come from, again?" I ask her, but she just stares at me, kinda blank. I try to say it again.

"Where . . ." I say, and I wave my hands around. "Do you"—I point to her—"come from?" I act out walking. But she just looks confused.

"No Anglisht," she says. And I'm thinking, How am I going to do this? But I don't have to worry about that anymore because finally Miss Salvato has gone inside. I know I'm being cold, but no way am I going to stand around talking to some weird girl I don't even like just to get on my teacher's good side. Not when my friends have got a rope going.

"Well, it's been real, but I got to run," I say, walking away.

Pretty soon, I'm right in the middle of the ropes, spinning around, touching the ground and then stomping from side to side like crazy.

"Go Maxie!" Brandee yells.

"Yeah, Maxie!" Tasha says.

"Go Maxie! Go Maxie! Go Maxie!" everyone else yells.

The more they're saying it, the faster I'm jumping till pretty soon my feet are just like a blur. When I'm done, Tasha comes over.

"You getting good, homey," Tasha says with her big smile.

"Thanks, homey," I say back.

Homey—that's a special word we got at my school for "friend." It's short for *homeboy* if your friend is a boy, or *homegirl* if your friend is a girl. When you call someone your homey, it's because they feel like a home to you, and you really like them. I'm lucky—I got a *lot* of homeys.

That's when I look up and notice the new girl. She's standing by the fence, digging her shoes into the ground and watching me. All alone.

5

DRITA

WHEN SCHOOL IS OVER, everywhere there are children and their families rushing to meet each other. I don't know where to look to find my mother, and I start to feel worried. But there waiting for me outside the school is Gjyshe. It seems so strange to see her there, wearing her old-fashioned *rrobe plake* and holding Hashim by the hand. My teacher shakes my hand and says something in English.

"*Gud beye, Drita. See yue tumarro,*" she says.

"Grandmother, where is Nënë?" I ask her because I thought my mother was the one who would be meeting me. My grandmother just shrugs.

"She is still much too tired from the trip. Come, Drita. Take your brother's hand. We must hurry for the bus."

Bus? No one said anything about a bus to me. But I follow

my grandmother through the doors and across the street. There is a big sign for the place where the bus will stop.

"Grandmother," I ask, "are you sure this is the right place to wait?"

"Yes, yes. Now come on!" she says because the big blue-and-white bus is coming down the street.

"But are you sure this is the right one?" I ask her again. "They are all different, you know!" I say, trying not to sound worried. Even in Kosova, my grandmother was not so good at going places by herself.

"Oh *zot*, Drita. You talk too much!" my *gjyshe* says, trying to hold Hashim's hand. But he is moving around too much and won't stay still.

"Bad boy!" scolds my grandmother.

Hashim puts his baby finger in his mouth and begins to cry. Now I know my grandmother must be worried. Usually she is more patient with my brother.

We climb up the steps, and my grandmother puts some money in the slot, just like in Kosova. It seems strange to me that even though everything in New York is different, the buses are exactly like the ones in my country.

"Up, up," my grandmother says, putting Hashim into a seat. My grandmother unfolds a little piece of paper and studies it. The words "112 Bedford Avenue" are written there in my father's handwriting. Our new home.

The bus turns down a street and we pass the market. In the morning, this colorful and noisy place made me happy, but now all I feel is worried.

Across from us there is a lady in a black jacket and a boy, a little older than my brother. They are staring at us.

"That lady looks nice, Gjyshe," I tell her. "We should ask her for help."

"She doesn't speak Albanian," my grandmother says.

"But if you show her the address, she might know!" I say back. "I know a few words. Maybe if she speaks slowly, I will understand."

But my grandmother shakes her head.

The little boy smiles at us, while his *nënë* looks out the window. From the way he is chewing, I can tell he has a big piece of gum in his mouth.

Now, more and more people get on the bus. But these people do not act friendly to us. They have dark faces and clothes. They stare at the floor or read the newspaper. Soon the bus is so crowded. I know my grandmother is lost.

At last, the lady grabs her son's hand and they stand up. I am worried that once they get off the bus, no one else will speak with us. But now we are lucky, because the nice lady comes over to us. She holds the metal rail and smiles down at us.

"*R u peepul last?*" she asks.

My silly grandmother is still staring ahead, afraid to speak to an American person. I know it is not so nice of me, but even if my grandmother is mad, I don't care. I take the paper from my grandmother's hands and show it to the lady. I try to remember some of the English words my father is teaching me.

"*Pleez,*" I say. "*Where is.*" The lady looks at the address.

"*Com,*" she says, waving her hand. "*Falloh me!*"

I almost have to pull my grandmother off the bus and down to the sidewalk.

"*Vat way,*" the nice lady says, pointing in one direction. "*Go varee far!*" Standing next to her, the little boy blows his bubble. POP it goes, and the pink candy is all over his face. If we were not so lost, maybe this boy would be a good friend for Hashim.

"*Thank yue,*" I say to the lady.

Now we begin our walking. First we walk ten blocks, then twenty.

"Oh *bo bo,* where is it?" my grandmother says.

"I think it's very far."

"But the sign says Bedford," poor Gjyshe says, still confused.

"Yes, but look—the numbers on the buildings are different," I tell her. "That means we are far away."

Soon, Hashim becomes so tired, I have to carry him in my arms.

"*Zot!*" my grandmother complains. "My feet are so sore."

Because it feels like now we are walking one hundred blocks. But then at last, we see the building that says 112. Our home.

My grandmother groans going up the stairs. "This city is too big for an old woman like me!"

I think my grandmother is right. This was too much walking for her—and for me too. If only my mother had come to meet me, we wouldn't have had such a bad time.

But when we open the door, I see that it is true: my mother is still too tired from the trip.

Because she is lying on the bed just like this morning, wrapped in a blanket. And she is fast asleep.

6

Maxie

WHEN I GET HOME AFTER SCHOOL, my whole house smells like chicken and dumplings.

"Mmm, Grandma, that sure smells good," I say, and I am real glad my grandma likes to baby me, after all.

"How was school?" she says. "Was your teacher mad you were late?"

"Not really," I say, trying not to meet her eye. It's best not to talk about anything else that happened today. Especially the part about back-talking my teacher.

"Now about this morning. Maxie, I really think you ought to give your daddy's friend a chance. Who knows, maybe you might decide that you—"

"Grandma, I'm going to say hello to my mama now," I say, cutting her off. If there's anything I don't want to do right now, it's talk about someone named Lisa.

My grandma's face gets real soft for a second, but she don't say nothing, just reaches her hand out to touch my chin.

"Sure, baby."

In my room, I have a little corner that is just my mother. First I have some pictures of her, all standing up in frames. I have her watch and her rings in a little glass dish that was hers, and a bottle of her favorite Prince Matchabelli perfume that my father said I can start wearing when I get old enough.

My mother died in a car accident three years ago. I was with her in the car, but I don't remember anything about it. All I remember was waking up in the hospital. At first they didn't tell me what happened, but then they did. I was seven and she was thirty-eight.

I pick up my favorite picture of her. It's the one of us together when I was a baby in the hospital. She looks tired and sweaty from having me and her hair is all messed, but her face looks so, so, so, so happy. I wish I could remember that day.

"Hi, Mama," I say, and I think about telling her the bad news—that my daddy has a new girlfriend maybe. But then I don't want to. Because if my mother knew something like that, maybe she wouldn't come back to me.

I know it's a stupid thing to think about. I know it's never really going to happen. But sometimes I still like to imagine what it would be like if my mother came back. Maybe I'd be sitting around watching TV and I'd hear a knock at the door. When I open it, it'll be her. Or one day I might be riding around on the train, and the lady next to me will smile and it'll be my mama's smile.

"I just had to see you, baby," she'll say. "Because I missed you so much."

"I missed you more, Mama," I'll tell her. "I missed you so much sometimes it hurt."

"Maxie!" my grandma calls from the other room. "I got a surprise for you."

When I come home in a sad mood, there's nothing can get me out of it, except one thing: sitting by my grandma's big leg, watching TV and eating popcorn. But I would never tell my grandma that. There's no telling how she would lord something like that over me. I think maybe she knows anyway because when I go in the living room there's my grandma sitting on the couch with a big bowl of popcorn on her lap. She even gives me the clicker.

"Now don't eat too much popcorn," she says. "I don't want you to spoil your appetite."

I'm just about to switch to Nickelodeon when the newscaster comes on to say: "Now we'll be hearing from our foreign correspondent in Kosovo."

"Hey," I say. "There's a girl in my class that comes from there."

"Well, for goodness' sake, turn it up!" she says.

I have to say, what we see next is kind of a shock to me because it looks like that place where Drita comes from is nothing but a war. The camera just keeps showing a lot of people running and buildings falling down and babies crying. Then they show some kind of marketplace where a bomb went off and some people lying on the ground look like they're dying, and that's when my grandmother takes the clicker from my hand.

"I think that's plenty of TV for tonight," she says.

"Dang, Grandma, it's not gonna upset me. I've seen worse stuff than that on MTV," I say.

"Don't curse!"

"I just said 'dang.'"

"Well, don't say it! It sounds like cussin'," she says, and I can tell there's no arguing with her. When my grandma makes up her mind about something, you just can't change it. She pulls herself up off the couch and goes into the kitchen, shuffling her feet across the rug in her old broken-down nurse's shoes. My grandma always complains she's got bad feet from almost thirty years of working as the head nurse at Roosevelt Hospital. That's why I saved up twelve dollars at Christmastime to buy her a nice cushy pair of slippers. Only problem is, she never wears them. Secretly, I think she likes those funky old nurse shoes better.

"Don't worry, baby, I'm saving those new moccasins

you gave me for a special occasion," she says, winking at me.

My grandma and me are about as close as we can be and in a lot of ways we're just the opposite. For one thing, she always thinks the things you see on TV are going to stay in your mind for a long time and ruin your brain. I think the things you see on TV hardly stay in your mind at all and might even make you smarter.

But tonight it seems like maybe she's right after all because I can't stop thinking about that news show all the way through homework time and then during dinner, so that I hardly taste my dumplings.

Finally, when I am in bed, Grandma comes in to shut the light off.

"Grandma, I made fun of her," I say when it's nice and dark.

"Who, baby?" my grandma says.

"That girl from Kosovo. But I'm not going to do it again."

"Is that why you got in trouble with your teacher?" she says.

"I swear, Grandma, you got ESP powers. How'd you know that?"

"Whenever my baby comes home telling me everything was 'fine,' I know it means no such thing."

"I'm glad you're so smart, Grandma."

"And I'm glad you learned your lesson, honey. You always got to be kind to people. Always. That's what your mama would want. Now, sleep tight," she says, and shuts the door.

I roll over on my side. Behind my eyes I see flashes of orange, look like bombs dropping, and I know my grandmother is right.

"Good night, Mama," I say, "good night."

7

DRITA

"HOW R YUE?" Mrs. Martinez says to the Chinese boy, Yang.

"Ah I fah," Yang says. Even I can tell he is forgetting too many sounds when he speaks. Mrs. Martinez touches Yang's face to show him how to make the sounds better.

Speaking English is very difficult—like moving rocks around inside your mouth using only your tongue. That is why after two days in my new school, I discover that I must have a special teacher, Mrs. Martinez. At first I did not like Mrs. Martinez. I was afraid of her long fingernails and her funny smell. I did not like her classroom either, with the yellow paint and small chairs meant for babies like Hashim, not ten-year-old children like me. But now I know Mrs. Martinez is just as nice as Miss Salvato, because she always gives you candy.

"How *ah* you today? I am fine," I say to the mirror. I

watch my mouth the way Mrs. Martinez shows me. If I work hard, maybe one day soon I can walk up to one of the American girls in my school and talk just like them.

Brandee is one girl in my regular class. Some others are Kayla, Evaliz, Tiffany and Jordania. One day I am hoping we can all be friends, but I have to speak better English first.

"*How r yue?*" I say, concentrating on the round "r" sound. I wonder why American has to be so different from my language.

Yang looks over at me and gives me a big smile. It's good to have boys as your friends, but as your *shoge të ngushtë*, your best friend, you must have a girl to tell your secrets to— secrets such as which boy in school is nicest, or what are your special dreams.

Here is the first secret I would tell my *shoge të ngushtë* if I had one: I still miss my friend Fitore so much.

In Kosova, Fitore lived in the same building with me. She has six brothers and with me there is only Hashim, so we became like sisters. Fitore's father is a famous writer in Kosova, so when the war came, it was very bad for them. Now they live in Australia, where it is safe for Albanian people. When I go home today, I will write her a letter. Maybe one day I can visit her.

Just thinking about Fitore makes me feel sad. I have not seen her for such a long, long time.

Mrs. Martinez comes over. I think she is noticing the look on my face.

"Drita, wot es va mater?" she asks.

I look over to make sure Yang is not listening. Even though he does not speak well, I do not like talking about private things with a boy nearby.

"Mrs. Martinez, I need *bafroom*," I tell her. To me, it seems strange that in America when you need to use the *tualet*, you must ask for a *banjë*—a bath instead.

Mrs. Martinez puts her hand on my shoulder.

"Ov curs, Drita. Take va pass," she says, and points to the wooden board with words on it that hangs by the door. For some reason, in an American school you must always carry this strange thing to the *banjë* when you go.

Mrs. Martinez smiles as I pass by her desk and slips a piece of orange candy in my pocket.

I walk down the hallway to the girls' room. But when I go in there, I see something that surprises me. There is a girl sitting on the *lavarnan*—the sink. She is a small, dark-skinned girl from my class whose name I do not know.

"Stap, who gooz vere?" she says, and her voice sounds loud in the *banjë*.

Quickly, I try to remember some American words to say back to her. But now I can't think of any.

"Moxee," she says and points to herself.

I try to smile at her.

Now the girl does something strange. She jumps off the sink and goes to the box on the wall. Out of the box she takes many papers. Now she puts them in the sink and turns on the water. Woosh goes the water, filling the sink.

I see what this girl is doing. She is making a flood. I am so surprised, I just stand there watching.

"*Giv me fihv,*" she says and reaches her hand to me.

This girl wants something, I think. But I have nothing to give her. Then I remember what it is in my pocket. I put the orange candy in her hand.

The girl looks surprised.

"*Thank yue!*" she says and smiles. For one moment, her smile makes this girl's face very beautiful, but then the smile is gone because now we hear a man's voice shouting "*Moxee Nikals!*" from outside the room.

I run out as fast as I can. Near the door is the man who is the boss of the school, the principal. He looks very angry.

I don't even mean to, but I start to feel afraid. As fast as I can, I go down the hallway to the ESL room.

"*Moxee Nikals!*" I hear the voice of the principal booming again, but I do not wait to see what will happen next. I slip through the door of my classroom and hang the wooden board on its nail. I take my seat again.

This crazy girl *Moxee,* I don't know what she's doing. But I know I don't like it.

8

Maxie

"DO YOU WANT TO EXPLAIN YOUR BEHAVIOR?" the principal says.

He's as mad as anything and he's got his hand right on the telephone. All I can think about is my daddy's face when he answers the telephone at work and he hears I'm in the principal's office again.

"Please don't call my daddy, Mr. Littman," I say, trying to hold back my tears.

"Do you realize the damage you could have caused? Who do you think would pay for that?"

"It was a mistake!" I say.

"A mistake? How can flooding the bathroom be a mistake? Are you saying you don't have any control over the things you do?"

"I do but . . . "

"But what? I don't understand how you could do that!"

39

Neither do I. Ever since second grade, I've had a problem in my school. I'll be going along every day, doing my work and having fun. But then one day I wake up and I get a bad idea in my head. In second grade, the idea I got was to write some words on the wall in permanent marker. Last year, my bad idea was to get Kayla to sneak into the auditorium with me. I was trying to teach her how to play "Chopsticks" on the school piano.

"Well?" he says. "Do you have anything to say for your-self?"

"I was trying to talk to her, Mr. Littman."

"Who?" he says.

"That new girl. Drita. Miss Salvato said I should find out about her for my social studies project. But she doesn't speak English. I thought maybe she'd laugh."

"Your job in school is not to make other people laugh, Maxie. We've discussed this before," he says.

"I know. I'm sorry. I won't do it again. Now are you going to call my father?"

Mr. L. takes a deep breath and sits back in his chair. He looks at me for a long time, like he's sizing me up.

"How is your dad? I haven't seen him much lately," he says finally.

I forget, sometimes, that Mr. Littman really helped my family a lot after the accident, and sort of got to be friends with my daddy. He even came to Mama's memorial and got me extra help in school when I was having a hard time concentrating on my work. That's why my daddy says Mr. Littman is tough, but fair. I just think he's tough. Either way he's the kind of teacher you better tell the truth to or else you'll *really* be in trouble.

"He has a new girlfriend named Lisa," I tell him.

"That's nice," says Mr. L. He doesn't look surprised at all. "Do you like her?"

"I didn't meet her yet. But I don't think so."

"Really? Why is that?" he asks.

I try hard to think of a reason why I wouldn't like someone I never even met before. I can only think of one.

"Usually I don't like people with that name," I say, but that's not really true. My third cousin is named Lisa and I like her just fine. But Mr. L. thinks about that for a minute.

"You know, Maxie, this school has rules."

"Yes, Mr. Littman."

"I'm not in the habit of bending them for any child," he says.

"I know, Mr. Littman."

"As far as I'm concerned, you are on probation. That is not a good thing."

"Yes, sir," I say.

"I have a book I'd like you to read." Now that surprises me.

"A book. You mean like for a report?"

"Maybe. But mostly I'd just like you to read it."

I can't believe my ears. Reading a book? That's so easy! Mr. L. reaches into his bag and puts the book on the table.

"Is it fiction or nonfiction?" I say, looking at it.

"Nonfiction. It was something I bought for myself. It's not really a children's book, however."

"I'm a pretty good reader, Mr. Littman," I say.

"I know. That's why I'm asking you. Think you can handle it?"

I pick up the book. It doesn't look so hard. There's lots of maps and photographs.

"Okay. But I got to ask you this—why?"

The principal just looks at me over his glasses, with that smart face of his.

"So you can learn something, of course."

9

DRITA

"NËNË," I say when I am coming home from school, "are you all right?"

It is still daytime outside, but in the living room of my house it feels like night with all the windows closed and dark. My mother lies on the old orange couch in her nightdress and slippers. Even in the dark, I can see her face looks like she's crying. I put my hand on her shoulder.

"I did a good job in school today, Nënë," I tell her, but my mother doesn't even seem to hear me, just lies back on the pillows and closes her eyes.

"I got a new math book. I think I know as much as anyone else. Maybe more. My teacher thinks I'm a smart girl," I tell her, but her face stays sad. "My English teacher says 'eggsellent' to me, Nënë. This is a word for good work."

I do not know what is wrong with my mother now that

she is in America. I do not know what is making her so different. Maybe in Kosova she was not so happy, but now that we are here, she lies on the couch all day, just wrapped in a blanket. Crying and sleeping, this is all she does now.

For a long time I cannot think of anything else to say, but finally I do. Too bad it is only a lie.

"I made many friends," I tell her. At last my mother opens her eyes.

"Oh, my *zemra ime*, I knew you would. How exciting! Tell me about them," she says finally.

"Well," I tell her, trying to keep the lying from my voice, "there is Evaliz. She has pretty eyes and interesting clothes like a rock star. And Kayla, who is small and very pretty. And then there is my favorite. Her name is Brandee. She is the best of all the girls. She is just like Fitore."

"Oh, Fitore," my mother says. "I remember her. She was so popular. Did she answer your letter?"

"Not yet, but Baba says mail from Australia takes a long time," I say, hoping I am right and that my friend Fitore has not forgotten me.

My mother lies back on the couch and soon she is sleeping again. I hear my grandmother's voice.

"Drita, come help me with dinner. We will let your mother rest," she says. Her voice has the same cheerful sound as always, but her eyes look troubled.

What is wrong with Nënë? Should we get a doctor? Why

does she lie in bed all day? These are the questions that are in my head all the time now, but they would be wrong to speak about. I do not wish to disobey my family by being too *guximtare*—too bold. Instead, my grandmother hands me the potato peeler. Tonight she is making special Albanian food to celebrate the good thing that is happening for my family—tomorrow my father will talk to an American company about a new engineering job.

"Drita, the potatoes are waiting for you!" my grandmother says when I come into the kitchen. Inside the big pot are the yellow potatoes I must peel and chop. Gjyshe is making her wonderful *byrek me mish*.

While I peel, my grandmother sprinkles the old wooden table with flour, brushing the white powder on the top. With one hand she grabs two handfuls of flour while the other hand cracks an egg into the center. Soon she is rolling the dough between her old fingers, rubbing and stretching it against the wood.

While she makes the crust, I watch and try to remember. Someday I will make *byrek me mish* and I will want to know my grandmother's secrets.

Gjyshe cuts the piece of soft dough and places it in the bottom of the dish. Now it is time for the potatoes and the green onions. My grandmother puts the dish in the oven.

Soon the whole house is full of the sweet smell of *byrek me mish* baking.

"Deleiciji!" my father says, sniffing the air, when he walks in.

"Drita," Gjyshe says. "Get the tray ready for your mother."

My grandmother has set four places at the table—for my father, my brother, herself and me—because lately my mother eats her dinner on the sofa, where she stays most of the time now. Many nights she eats very little—just one or two bites. I don't know how my mother can live eating so little, but my grandmother says not to worry. She says Mother eats when she is hungry, sometimes late at night after we go to sleep. But I don't know if I believe her.

"Never mind about that," says a voice. We look up and there is my mother standing in the doorway. She is holding her old robe around her neck and her brown hair is wild, but her face is smiling.

"Byrek me mish," she says. "I remember that smell from my childhood."

"Dashi!" my father says, jumping up. "We thought you were resting."

"I have been resting all day. Now it is time to wake up," says Nënë.

"I helped Gjyshe with the *byrek me mish*!" I tell her.

"Wonderful!" says my mother.

Hashim is so excited, he is running in circles around her feet.

"My little bear," Nënë says, picking him up. The look on

my brother's face is surprised when she holds him. Nënë does not hold him so much now, I think.

My father pulls a chair out for her. Soon we are all eating together. The *byrek me mish* my grandmother made is so good that even my mother seems happy, laughing and giggling like her old self.

"To my new job in America!" my father says, and we all raise our cups, even little Hashim.

I am so happy, I cannot stop smiling. Inside I know it is finally happening. The good life my family will have in America is finally beginning.

10

Maxie

HERE ARE SOME OF THE THINGS I find out about Kosovo from the book the principal gave me. It's a city that was once part of a country called Yugoslavia. For a long time, the boss of Yugoslavia was a guy named Tito. Tito wasn't a good guy, but he kind of kept things together. But when Tito died, the Serbians were the people who got to be in charge of Kosovo. The problem was, not everyone thought it was their city. The Albanians had been there a long time and they thought it was theirs too.

And that's as far as I get when my dad says, "Honey, I'd appreciate it if you'd put that book down. We're trying to have a conversation here."

Even though his voice is as sweet as sugar, something tells me he's not playing. I put the book down, but I'm not real happy about it because now instead of reading about something interesting, I'm sitting at the Lobster Pound Restaurant with my dad, his annoying girlfriend Miss Thing Lisa and her annoying son Darrell.

"Vroom vroom," goes Darrell. He's got all these Transformer toys spread out all over the tablecloth. With his little buzz haircut and his Yankees shirt, everyone probably thinks he's as cute as cute can be, but to me he's just a pain.

Miss Thing clears her throat. "So, Maxine . . . are you working on a report for school?" she says in that squeaky voice of hers.

Her hair is done up in a wave, and she's wearing gold earrings that have a script "L" in them for "Lisa." Her whole look is trashy in my opinion. Even worse, her hand is resting on my daddy's arm like she owns him or something.

"Yes," I say about as flat as I can manage.

"Is it interesting?" she says.

"Not really," I lie.

"Knock, knock," goes Darrell.

"Who's there?" my daddy says.

"Thumping," he says, already starting to crack himself up.

"Thumping who?" Miss Thing answers. I guess my daddy forgot to tell them how much I hate knock, knock jokes.

"Thumping green and slimy is crawling up your neck!" he says.

"Daddy," I say when they stop laughing. "I got to be home by nine so I can watch my show."

"Maxie, we just got here," he says with a smile still on his face.

"But I really, really want to see my show. Daddy, you know how much I love it," I remind him.

"We'll see," he says, and now his smile looks kind of annoyed.

"But . . ." I say.

"I said we'll see!" he goes, gritting his teeth together. If he's not careful, he's gonna get one of his bad headaches.

"So, Gerald. What's happening with the promotion?" Miss Thing asks, changing the subject to the fancy new job my dad is going to get at his bank. And then off they go, talking on and on about my daddy's job like I'm not even there.

Darrell looks at me and smiles, but that only puts me in a worse mood.

Stupid kid, I think to myself. But here comes the waitress with some food before I die from boredom.

"Mmmm, shrimp cocktail!" I take two big pink shrimps even though my daddy only ordered one appetizer to share with the whole table. Now there's four left. Miss Thing and Daddy each take one and so does Darrell.

"Yum!" he says, stuffing his face. There's one shrimp left.

Did you ever get a feeling that something bad's going to happen, only you don't know what it is? Well, I get that feel-

50

ing all the time. Like, for instance, the day I broke my toe. I knew something bad was going to happen and bingo—a plaque of the Ten Commandments fell off my grandmother's wall and landed on my foot, just like that.

Sitting there, looking at those wooden lobster traps and plastic lobsters they got all over the walls there, I get my feeling that some real bad disaster is about to happen.

That's right when Darrell grabs the last shrimp.

"Hey!" I say. "That was *mine!*"

"But you already had two!" He pouts.

"Chump," I say in my meanest way.

"Huh?" says Darrell.

"Maxie!" says my daddy.

"You a chump!"

"Mommy, what's a chump?" whines Darrell. Now that *really* cracks me up.

"Ha, ha! You such a chump you don't even know what a chump is!" And I'm laughing so hard, I almost fall off my chair.

"Waaaaaa!" cries Darrell.

"Maxie!" says my daddy so loud that people two tables away turn around to look at us.

Then the waitress comes with the rest of our food.

"Yum, lobster!" I say. But my daddy only stands up. He puts on his coat.

"That's all right," he says to the waitress. "We'll take ours to go."

11

DRITA

"DRITA, TAKE THE FOUL SHOT!" says Kayla, smiling at me.

"You can do it!" says Brandee.

"Sink the ball and you will have all the friends," says the other girl, Shonte.

I am at my school, PS 18, and I am playing basketball. But what is strange to me is the size of the gym. It is like a gigantic canyon with the basketball hoop at one end of it.

"I have not played since I was in Kosova!" I tell them.

Now I am surprised to see Fitore there.

"Fitore? What are you doing here?" I ask her.

"Don't you remember, Drita? I go to this school too!" she says. "Take your shot!"

I aim at the hoop and throw the ball. I am so surprised to see that it lands in the hoop.

"Yeah, Drita!" the girls shout. "You are a championship player!"

And that is when I wake up from my nice dream.

On the side of the bed where my *gjyshe* was sleeping, the covers are thrown back and the bed is empty.

"Gjyshe?" I say in the dark. "Where are you?" But my grandmother doesn't answer.

In Prishtina, I had my own room full of toys and posters of American singers, but in America I have to share a bed with my grandmother. At first, this was something for me to complain about, but the truth is, I like it. Because now when I wake up in the middle of the night, it's not so lonely.

"Gjyshe?" I say again, but no one answers.

Then I hear something and sit up straight in bed. Some-one screaming. Loud.

"Gjyshe? Nënë? What is happening?" I say.

"Yaaaaaa!" goes the screaming again. This time I recog-nize the voice.

I jump out of my bed and run to my mother's room.

"Nënë! Nënë! What's wrong?" I say.

When I open the door, the lights are on and my father is standing by the window. My grandmother is sitting on the bed, patting my mother's head. My mother's eyes are closed, but she is crying so much.

"What's wrong with her?" I ask. "Is she sick?"

"Sshh, Drita, she is still sleeping," my father says.

Sleeping? How can she be sleeping? With all that noise?

"It's a nightmare. She dreams about Cousin Zana," my grandmother says.

"You don't know that," says Baba.

"Yes, I do, she told me," Gjyshe replies.

"Go back to bed, Drita," my father says. "Grandmother will stay here with Nënë tonight. I have to work in a few hours anyway."

It all seems very strange to me to be woken up from my nice dream by my mother's nightmare, but I am too sleepy to ask more questions.

When I go back inside my room, Hashim is standing in his crib, looking at me with big eyes. I think he is scared too.

"Sshh, baby, don't be frightened," I tell him. "It was just a bad dream that Nënë had."

My brother reaches his arms toward me. There is still sleep in his face and tears also.

"Poor baby, do you want to sleep with me?" I say, picking him up. It feels good to have a little warm person in the bed with me, not so lonely.

Soon, Hashim is sleeping peacefully, his fingers in my hair.

"*Gjumë të embël,* baby," I whisper in his ears. In Albanian that means "sweet sleep."

I close my eyes, and I try to find my own nice dream again. Too bad for me, it is gone.

12

Maxie

"I HAVE NEVER BEEN SO EMBARRASSED IN ALL MY LIFE!" my father says as soon as we get back in the car.

Now I know my bad feeling was right; something bad *did* happen at dinner. The only problem is—it wasn't just an accident. The bad thing was me—my attitude.

"I'm sorry, Daddy," I say, and I am. But my daddy is too mad to listen.

"Just answer me one thing," he says finally. "Why'd you have to make that child cry?"

"He took the last shrimp!" I say.

"You called him a chump!" he says. As if I don't remember.

"Well, he shouldn't have done that!"

"He's four years old, Maxie. You're ten."

"So?" I say. "So what! He was being rude!"

"No, he was being a little kid. You're supposed to be the mature one, but you acted just the same as he did. Worse! Maxie, when are you going to grow up?" he says.

"Don't yell at me, Daddy!" I say because his voice is filling up the whole car.

"I'll yell at you if I want to yell at you!" he yells.

Even though he's right, I really hate getting yelled at. It makes me say the meanest thing I can think of back to him.

"You don't want her to come back," I say.

"Come back?" my daddy asks. For a second he's so surprised, he almost swerves the car.

"Come back? Maxie? What do you mean by that?"

"Mama. If she came back, you wouldn't even want her to. You'd just want what's-her-name as your girlfriend. 'Cause she's young and pretty."

"Is that what you really think?"

"Yes . . . no . . . I don't . . . not really," I say.

"Maxie." Now Daddy's voice is gentle, not mad. "I think about your mother every day. I pray for her up in heaven. I'd give everything to have her back, even for one day. But that's never going to happen. Never."

I put my head against the window. It feels nice and cold, like a cool hand against my face. It feels like her hand.

"Honey . . ." my daddy says and I know he's trying to get me to see things his way. "Your mother is gone. Do you understand that?"

"Yes, I understand that but . . . " I say.

"But what, Maxie?" he asks.

There's a sound in his voice like pain when he says it, and I can't even look at him because I know how much he loved her too. I know I shouldn't say it because it's a bad and jealous thought, but I'm in a bad and jealous mood.

"How come Darrell gets to have his mother and I don't?"

My father sighs real heavy. For a second I think he's gonna cry too, but he don't.

"I wish I could answer that question," is all he says.

13

DRITA

IN THE LUNCHROOM, I stand by the garbage cans and I watch them. The American girls: Evaliz, Brandee and Kayla. Of course, today I notice Brandee the most because of the way she wears her hair, like a crown on her head. It was right what I tell my mother. Brandee is like Fitore: *ka shoge shumë*—very popular. If I can make her my friend too, then all the other girls will like me.

Then I see the empty seat next to her. I rush over.

I make the words as carefully as I can. "Hello, Brandee!" I say, and put my bag down.

"Hello, Brandee!" I say again in a louder voice. At first she does not answer because she is talking to her friend, but then she looks at me. In her mouth she has a straw and some of her red juice has spilled on her chin.

I open my lunch box. Inside is the *byrek me mish* wrapped in foil. I take it out.

"Brandee, will you *chare wif* me?" I say in my best English.

All the girls stop and look at what I have put on the table.

Now all the talking stops.

Brandee takes her finger and she points it at the *byrek me mish* that I try to give her. On the end of each fingernail, she has a pink flower painted, just like a girl in *Young Miss* magazine. But the look on Brandee's face is not friendly at all.

Brandee picks up the *byrek me mish* in her hand and squeezes it. The good potato filling comes out all over the table. Now she takes a handful and throws it backward over her head.

Splat! A big piece of *byrek me mish* lands on one boy's jacket. The boys turn around at once.

The boy in the coat is yelling. In his hand, he is holding something. Brandee and the other bad girls are under the table when he throws it.

Something wet goes into my hair.

"*Yak!*" Brandee screams.

"*Gros!*" Evaliz says.

"Hahahaha!" they all shout.

How stupid of me to bring my Albanian food into an American school. How stupid of me to think that these girls would ever like me. No one does, and no one ever will.

But I don't cry. I just get up from the table and go to clean myself off. I think some of those boys got in trouble, but I don't even care. All day my hair smells bad.

I am so glad when the day is over and I see my father waiting for me in front of school. Until my grandmother learns more about the buses, my father has decided he should be the one to meet me after school.

"Good afternoon, Drita," Baba says in English. "How was school?"

"*Çka,*" I answer him. In our language that means "so-so." I don't feel so much like speaking American today. Across the backseat, his good brown jacket is crumpled in a ball. I remember about the *intervistë* he has today.

"Baba, what has happened with the new job?" I ask him.

My father does not look at me, just shrugs his shoulders. Now I know today was not a good day for him either and he did not get the job.

For one second I feel like I am going to cry, but then my father turns up the radio. I can hear the voice of the American *gazetar* talking about our country.

"What are they saying?" I ask. My father's English is better than mine, so he can understand the words.

"They are talking about the United Nations," my father tells me. "Some people are saying that the Americans and the UN will send soldiers to Kosova to keep the peace."

"But what does it mean?" I ask. "Is that a good thing?"

"Yes, it could be," he says.

"Do you think Cousin Zana is safe?"

"I don't know, Drita."

"But Nënë is so worried about that."

"I know, but there's nothing we can do. Miss Mirfue checks every day on the computer. All we can do is hope."

Suddenly, I feel so bad about everything. I can't stop the tears that are coming to my eyes.

My father turns the mirror so he can see my face. I think now he notices my dirty hair.

"Poor Drita, did you have a hard day?" he asks.

"Yes," I tell him. "Oh, Baba, what are we going to do? You didn't get the job and that school is so hard for me."

"Zot, Drita, we have to do what the Albanian people always do when things are difficult," he says. "Next time, we must try harder."

14

Maxie

"Look at her," Brandee says, "stuck up."

"She thinks she's alla that," Kayla says.

"What's she following us around for?" says Miss Sha, otherwise known as Shonte.

"Would you be quiet already, you're going to make me miss my shot," I say.

It's recess and we're in the yard. I close one eye and focus on the sweet spot my daddy told me about. It's on the backboard, right above the basket. I take my time, aim and throw.

The ball flies through the air like a rocket, taps the board real light and spins into the basket with a big swoosh. I've always been good at sports. Who knows, maybe one day I'll wind up playing for the New York Liberty.

"All right, now," goes Brandee. "Enough showing off. Let's choose up sides."

Shonte runs off to get Tasha and Tiffany B. for Kayla and Brandee's team. On my side, it's April, Emani, Jordania, me and Tiffany M.

"Let's play," Brandee says, slapping the ball away from April and dribbling it between her legs. When it comes to b-ball, that Brandee is the world's biggest hot dog.

"But Jordy can't play," Emani says.

Jordania nods her head. "Yeah, I hurt my hand in music class."

That's a real shame for us because ever since she went to basketball camp last summer, Jordania's been everyone's top player after me and Brandee.

"I don't want to play if it's four against five. It ain't fair," says Tiffany M.

That's when Drita steps up.

"I play," she says.

"Forget it, Drita Draino," Brandee says.

Boy, I'm wishing I never thought up that stupid joke. But Drita looks her right in the eye.

"I play," she goes again and reaches for the ball. Brandee knocks her hand away. Hard.

"Hands off, scrub," Brandee says.

In case you want to know, "scrub" is a name we use for someone who's new to basketball and doesn't know anything. It's kind of like an insult. Well, not kind of. It *is* an insult.

Drita looks at me.

"C'mon, Brandee," Jordy says. "Who knows, maybe they got basketball in Russia."

"They don't got no basketball in Russia, dope. She ain't playing," Brandee says.

If there's one thing I hate, its being bossed around. Especially by someone think she knows everything, like Brandee.

"For the one thing, the girl don't come from Russia. She comes from Kosovo. For another, I'm the captain of this team and I say she can be on my side," I say back.

"Fine. Whatever. We still gonna beat you," sniffs Brandee.

"That's right!" says Kayla.

"Jordy, you the ref, throw out," Brandee says, tossing her the ball.

I look over at Drita. One thing she got going for her is her height. She's tall and thin, and looks more like a fifth grader than a fourth grader. And for a basketball scrub, she doesn't look nervous at all.

"You be the point guard. You know what that is?"

But Drita don't say nothing, just grits her teeth and watches as Jordy throws the ball high into the center of the court.

Smack! goes the ball. Brandee whacks it away from

Emani. Tasha scoops up the ball. She may be little, but she's fast. She dribbles it close to the ground and passes to Kayla.

"Just try to keep the ball away from Brandee," I yell to my homeys.

Unfortunately, that's right when Kayla passes back to Brandee.

My daddy says that there are two kinds of players in basketball: the kind that shares the ball and plays for the good of the whole team, and the kind that hogs the ball so that they can get all the glory for themselves. Brandee definitely falls into the last category.

Homegirl fakes like she's gonna pass to someone, but instead, she goes right and then left. Now Tasha, Shonte, Tiffany and Kayla all rush in behind her, blocking my girls. Now none of us can get to Brandee and it looks like she's got a free shot at our basket.

But then out of nowhere, there's Drita, coming in after Brandee from the other side. Brandee fakes to the side but Drita stays with her, crouching over her and bumping into her with her leg. Everywhere Brandee moves, there is Drita, with a lot of scrambling going on between the rest of us.

"Check out the scrub!" says Tiffany.

"You go, girl!" yells Emani.

"Stay on her, Drito!" Jordy says from the sidelines, and no one notices she got Drita's name wrong.

"Get out of my face!" Brandee yells, because finally someone is making her work and she's not used to that.

But Brandee's still got some surprise moves left. She ducks fast under Drita's arm and makes a shot at the basket. The ball flies toward the net, but misses and rebounds off of the backboard.

Kayla, Brandee, me and Tasha make a rush for the ball, but Drita's there first. She practically takes the ball away right out from Brandee's hands. But Drita's in a bad position. She's boxed in by Tasha and Kayla now. She passes to me. I take a couple of steps back and pass to Tiffany M. Bam! Tiffany scores.

"Great assist!" I yell at Drita.

"Wooah! What defense!" says Emani, slapping her hand.

But now Brandee's screaming too.

"That girl hit me with her elbow!" she yells.

"Did not!" Emani yells back.

"Wait a second," Jordania says. "I'm the ref and I saw the whole thing. She didn't touch you."

"You lie!" Brandee howls.

"It was a foul!" Kayla says.

"Jerk!" Brandee screeches. "Cheater!"

"Stop, stop!" I yell, trying to get in between them, because now Brandee is all up in Drita's face. She smacks Drita hard, right across the cheek.

"What are you doing?" I yell.

"Get your hands off me, Maxie!" she screams, because I got her by the shirt.

But I'm so mad, I can't even think about what I'm doing. I hit Brandee hard right in the stomach.

"Ow!" Brandee yells. She's sitting in the dirt with tears coming down her face.

"See how you like it, you bully!" I scream at her. All my friends' faces look shocked. They back away from me like, Who you gonna hit next? I turn around to see where Drita went, but she's gone.

Across the yard comes Miss Salvato.

15

DRITA

WHEN I AM LIVING IN KOSOVA and there's a war, I always have one big worry. I am afraid that I will be a *frikacake*. For an Albanian person, this is the worst thing to be—a coward. Even children should fight back.

But when Brandee hits me, I can't. I can't move, or make a fist. I can't raise my arm to hit her back. All I can do is stand there with my hands at my side.

"Yaaaaa!" they are all screaming around me. It hurts my face where Brandee hits me. But the sound they make hurts more—like fire alarms going off inside my ears. Brandee is shouting loudest of all. I know she is saying names about me.

"Stop, stop!" another girl yells back. It is the small girl from the *banjë*. I know her name too. Maxie.

And then she punches Brandee hard. I don't know why

she does this for me. Maybe they just hate each other, these American girls. Maybe they like to fight.

In Kosova, I have seen many fights. One time I saw some Serbian soldiers kicking a man on the street so much that he had blood coming out of his mouth. But even though I know this fight is not like that, it seems just as bad to me.

So when my teacher blows her whistle to stop, I don't listen like I am supposed to. Instead, I run past the fighting girls, into my school, down the hall and to the girls' *banjë*. I will hide there till lunch is over. I will hide all day if I have to.

I will not make my shame worse by letting them see me cry.

16

Maxie

"SHE HIT ME, MR. LITTMAN! She hit me!" Brandee yells, pointing her ugly finger at me. "I fell down and ripped my best pants too. My mom's gonna be mad!"

"Shut up about your stupid mother," I say back.

"Don't bust on my mother!" Brandee screams.

"I'll bust on your mother if I want to bust on your mother!" I yell.

"Sit down, both of you, and lower your voices," Mr. Littman commands. So me and Brandee sit down on opposite ends of the couch in his office because now instead of being my good friend since second grade, Brandee is my worst enemy.

"I would like to hear what happened," he says. "Now, who is going to go first?"

I'll give you three guesses who that's gonna be.

"Me and Kayla were just playing a game and-and-and-and she come and-and-and-and she hit me! And then when she hit me she laugh, Mr. Littman! She laugh at me!" Brandee says.

"Is that true, Maxie?" Mr. L. asks me.

So now I tell him what *really* happened: how Brandee was beating up Drita for no reason, and I tried to stop her.

"It was an accident!" Brandee screeches.

"Ask Miss Salvato, Mr. Littman, if you don't believe me. She saw everything that happened," I say.

"I plan to," says Mr. Littman.

Now Brandee opens her big mouth. "But that girl ruined our game," Brandee howls. I just knew she was going to get herself in trouble.

"If you hit Drita," Mr. Littman says, "then this is a very serious matter, Brandee. You know how I feel about bullying."

"Ha! Ha!" I say right in Brandee's face because she deserves it. But I guess that's a mistake because now Mr. Littman turns his X-ray eyes on me.

"I wouldn't feel too confident if I were you, Maxie. Hitting is not allowed at PS 18 for any reason."

"Are you going to call my house?" I ask him because now it's my turn to be shaking in my shoes.

"You know the rules."

Unfortunately for me, I do.

17

DRITA

WHEN I ARRIVE HOME, the sound of the American news show fills my house.

"Hello, Gjyshe, hello, Nënë," I say. I try to speak loudly so they will hear me above the television set.

"Ah, Drita, here you are at last. Let me fix you something," my grandmother says, getting up from the couch. "Go speak to your mother."

I put away my coat and join my mother.

"Nënë, why is the television so loud?" I ask her.

My mother's eyes follow Gjyshe from the room. "Drita, I was watching Zana."

"Zana?" I ask her.

"Yes, she was on the television. She said things are very bad for her in Kosova."

"Really?" I say, feeling so confused about this. Why would

my cousin be on television? But before I can question her, Nënë asks me about my day.

"How are all your friends?" she says.

For one moment, I think I will tell my mother everything. But then I notice her face. Just speaking about my school makes her worried look go away.

"Today we played basketball," I tell her because at least that part is not a lie.

"I am so happy for you," my mother says.

Now my grandmother comes in with a glass of milk and some *biskota* for me.

"Gjyshe, Drita is doing so well at her new school. Aren't you proud of her?" my mother asks.

"Oh, Dashi! I am always proud of my Drita," my grandmother says, handing me my snack. She smiles at me too.

For the rest of the day and until bedtime, I think this is my hardest job, to hide the truth from my family.

Finally, when nighttime comes and I am in my bed, I think my bad day is over, and my lies too, but then my grandmother comes into the room.

"Are you awake?" she whispers.

In the dark, I can see her long gray hair resting on her shoulders like a girl. The night makes her old white nightgown into a purple one.

Gjyshe slides herself into the bed next to me. I close my eyes and roll onto my arm, like I am still sleeping.

"Come now, Drita, stop pretending, I know you're awake," Gjyshe says.

From the living room, now I hear the sounds of the comedy shows. A child makes a joke and then there is the sound of laughter. This is how it is on all the programs: families smiling and laughing and hugging one another.

"How did you know?"

Gjyshe smiles at me, breathing out her old smell, like lemons. Even with no lights, I can see the dark place in her smile where her tooth is missing. My grandmother used to have a fake tooth before the war, but I like her old smile better.

"What is wrong, *zemra?*" she says. Suddenly, I feel tears coming to my eyes.

"Oh, Gjyshe, they were so mean to me in the school," I say, and then I tell about playing basketball and the big fight. I talk for a long time and while I am talking, my grandmother listens, a serious look on her face.

"What kind of school is this with so much hitting?" she says.

"No. You're not supposed to do that," I explain. "You get in trouble for that."

"So these girls got in trouble? For fighting?"

"Yes, I think so."

"Listen, I think you are a brave girl," she says finally. "Other children would not even try to make a friend."

"What does that matter?" I say. "They don't like me."

"What about this one girl, the one who helped you?" she asks. "Maybe she likes you. She did a good thing for you, I think."

I think about Maxie and what she did.

"Well, she did talk to me a few times. But she's so different from me," I tell her.

"Of course she's different. Who would want to be friends with someone just the same as themselves? It would be as interesting as looking in a mirror. But maybe inside this girl is just like you—full of ideas and plans."

"All right. Tomorrow I will talk to her. But please, don't tell Nënë what happened," I beg her, "she thinks I have lots of friends."

"You shouldn't deceive your parents, Drita."

Now I remember something I want to ask my grandmother.

"Gjyshe, was Zana really on the TV set?" I ask her.

"Who told you that?" Gjyshe asks.

"Nënë," I tell her.

A troubled look passes over my grandmother's old face.

"Your mother has been upset. Her imagination is playing tricks on her," she says.

"You see? That's why I can't upset her more. She has been so sad lately. Please, Gjyshe. Don't tell Nënë about the fight," I beg her.

My grandmother sighs.

"All right, Drita. I promise you. But now you must get some sleep. Tomorrow will be a better day. You will see," she says, kissing me good night.

Now I am so tired, I can't stop the yawning that comes on me.

"*Natën e mirë*, my Drita," Gjyshe whispers. Soon I am asleep.

18

Maxie

SO ME AND BRANDEE get the same punishment for fighting, which is: benched for two weeks. "Benched" is what they call it at my school when you get no recess or yard time and you have to sit on the bench near the principal's office. Let me tell you, that's no fun because after a while that bench feels *hard* on your behind.

After Mr. Littman called my house, my grandma decided I needed consequences at home too. So now I got no TV, playdates or phone privileges for two whole weeks either.

And that's not the worst part. The worst part is, I didn't even get to talk to my daddy about it because he's been so busy with work. I don't even want to know what he's going to say about everything.

"I guess the next two weeks won't be much fun," I say to myself. But then I notice someone walking over to me.

It's Drita.

"Hello, Maxie," she says.

"Hey! That sounds pretty good," I tell her because just for a second her English sounded almost normal. I think of something I've been wanting to ask her.

"Where'd you learn to play basketball?" I say, but she just looks at me and shrugs because she doesn't understand. Then I get this idea of how I can talk to her better. I go over to Gladys the yard lady.

"Maxie, you're benched," she says before I can even open my mouth.

"I know, Gladys, but I really, really, really need to get a book from my classroom pretty please with sugar on top! It's for a report!" You're not really supposed to go back to your classroom once it's recess-time, especially if you're benched. Good thing for me, Gladys is a friend of mine. We always crack each other up with jokes and stuff.

"Okay," Gladys says. "You got two minutes."

It's four flights up to my classroom, but I swear I get there in one minute.

"Knock, knock," I say, peeking inside the door for my teacher.

I remember when I was in second grade, it was always kind of a shock to me when I found out teachers drove around in cars and went to the supermarket just like regular people. But even though I know teachers are just like everyone else, it's still sometimes weird when you see them doing things like eating lunch or shopping. That's why I feel a little shy, suddenly seeing Miss Salvato sitting there, eating her lunch with her buddy Mr. Lee, the music teacher.

"Hello, Maxie," my teacher says, smiling.

"To what do we owe the pleasure of your company?" says Mr. Lee, because he's like that.

"I just gotta get something out of my book bag," I tell them.

I dig around inside the coat closet till I find it—the Kosovo book Mr. Littman gave me. Miss Salvato looks curious.

"What have you got there?" Miss S. asks.

I show her.

"The principal gave it to me so I can find out more about Kosovo for my social studies report."

"What a great idea!" she says.

"I'm starting to be friends with Drita too."

"How fabulous!" she says. The smile she gives me is so big, it lights up the place.

19

DRITA

When Maxie sits back down, I am so surprised to see what she is carrying, I almost fall off the bench.

"*Qyqja!*" I say in Albanian, when I see the book.

"*Wachoo say?*" says Maxie. Now she shows me the cover of the book. On it is a picture of the beautiful Balkan mountains, and the city Prishtina beneath them. KOSOVO, it says in English. You can tell this book was written by someone who was not Albanian because my people call my country "Kosova."

"*Mi hohm,*" I tell her.

"*I no,*" she says.

I open the pages. Inside there are pictures of my homeland, and many words. I wish that I could read them all to know what the writer is saying.

When I came to this school, I never thought anyone would

like my country or knows things about it. Now I find out I am wrong. Maxie reaches over and turns the page. There is a picture of a Serbian soldier pointing a gun. She points to it.

"*Wot's it like?*" she says.

But I don't think I know the English words for what she wants to know, so much.

"*Ushtar,*" I say in my language.

"*Ushtar,*" she says back. It sounds so strange to me to hear an American person pronounce an Albanian word.

"*Ushtar, ushtar, ushtar,*" Maxie says again. The way she says it, it makes the word "soldier" sound like a silly song.

"*Ushtar, ushtar, ushtar,*" she says more times because now we are both laughing.

Maxie takes out a paper. Then she says something to me that I do not understand.

"*Ex-yuz mee?*" I say back. Maxie pretends dial the *telefon*.

"*Drita, rit yur nambur,*" she says.

On the paper I write my name and our *telefon* number. Then I remember something else, another message to write.

Maxie watches me while I add some words to the paper. It takes me a little time because I want the spelling to be correct.

I put the paper in her hand. Maxie looks at it carefully. Then she gives me a big smile.

"*Shur,*" she says.

"Drita and Maxie. Friends, please" is what I am writing.

20

Maxie

"ARE YOU SURE YOU DON'T WANT TO COME WITH ME?" my grand-mother asks, standing in the doorway. She's got her purse and her new church hat on her head.

"That's okay, Grandma. I've got work to do." Of course, I wouldn't go to a Bible study class to save my life, but I'm not about to tell her that.

"Your daddy should be home in a little while. Now don't you dare turn on that TV. And no phone calls either. Re-member. You promised."

"And a promise is a promise," I say.

"That's right," she says like she's finally satisfied.

Behind my back, I uncross my fingers. My grandma doesn't know I made another promise today too. I promised I would be Drita's friend, and the only way to do that right now is by going against my grandma.

"Of course, Grandma," I say, not looking up.

My grandma pauses with her hand on the doorknob. I can tell she doesn't one hundred percent believe me, but she got nothing to pin on me.

I wait until I can hear the door close and the elevator going down before I dial.

"A'lo?" a voice on the telephone says.

"Is Drita home?" I say.

"Cfa re?" the voice says.

I tell myself that I'm not breaking the law—I'm only bending it. Because I also have a school reason to talk to Drita. After all, I'm supposed to be writing that report.

"Drita. Is. Drita. Home?" I say again.

There's a clank as Drita's mom or whoever it is puts down the phone and a lot of yelling and somebody's baby crying in the background. Then there's a long pause and I'm practically falling asleep I'm waiting so long. Finally someone picks up the phone.

"Who?" a man's voice says. That's it—just "Who?"

"Hello. This is Maxine Nichols. Is Drita there?" I say.

"Maxine Nichols?" he says, sounding sort of confused.

"I'm her friend, from school," I say slowly, and inside I'm starting to feel like this is a big mistake.

"What you want?" he says. I'm just about to ask if Drita's there when I hear something that sends electric shock waves all over my body.

It's the sound of the key in the front door.

Fast as I can, I hang up the phone, jump onto the bed and grab my book just as my grandmother comes back through the door.

"Get a lot of reading done?" she asks.

"Well, you're back pretty fast," I say. My heart is pounding so hard, it's a wonder she can't hear it. "Did you forget something, Grandma?"

My grandmother sits down and just looks at me.

"Well," she says at last, "are you going to 'fess up now, or later?"

I put my face in the pillow, and concentrate on that book. Too bad it wasn't a little bit more interesting, then I might not be in trouble.

"What do you mean?"

"I called from the phone in the lobby."

I'm so shocked, for one second I forget that it was me breaking my promise. My own grandmother, spying on me!

"Maxine. The line was busy."

"It was a wrong number," I say, thinking fast. My grandmother just looks at me, with that face of hers.

"It was!" I say.

"You are grounded, Maxine. That is not allowed. And you promised," my grandmother says. Loud.

"It was school-related."

"Maxine, I never thought I'd see the day that I'd say this to you, but I just don't believe you."

"It was. I was calling that girl Drita. For my report," I tell her, almost crying.

My grandmother just sits there, her big face like a rock, turned against me.

"It was that Kayla."

"It wasn't, I swear!"

"You sure?" she says. My grandmother doesn't like Kayla too much after we got in trouble last year for sneaking into the auditorium.

"Absolutely positive," I say, ready to swear on a stack of Bibles.

"All right, then. Go ahead. Make your call."

Even though I'm feeling like a real jerk for hanging up on Drita's daddy like that, I'm not about to argue. I dial the phone. Drita picks up on the first ring, like she's been waiting.

"*Jam Drita,*" she says.

"Hello, Drita, this is Maxie," I say.

"Oh, Maxie," says Drita, "hello."

If you think it's hard having a conversation with someone who doesn't speak English in person, try doing it on the phone while your grandmother is sitting right beside you, mad as anything, listening to every word. I ask her a few questions like how old she is and where she comes from and all of that. But then finally we run out of things to talk about.

"Well, I got to go now. Good-bye," I say, and I hang up the phone. Now my grandmother really starts with me.

"That's the problem with a lie, Maxie," she says. "It covers up your bad stuff and your good stuff too. That was a kindness you did, calling that girl. I would have let you call her if you'd just asked me. Why do you have to hide things, Maxie? It's not like you."

I can't really think of no answer to that, so I say, "That's just the way I am, I guess."

"Don't go telling me that's just the way you are. I know exactly how you are. You only started acting like this since you lost your mama. You got to start to let her go, Maxie."

"I don't know what you're talking about," I say, playing dumb. I hate it when my grandmother talks like this.

"That's only 'cause you don't want to. Let me ask you this. In the two years since the accident did you ever tell even one of your girlfriends that your mama passed? And don't say 'none of your business,' because I'm making it my business."

I shut my mouth because "mind your business" is exactly what I was going to say.

"It's not right, you hanging on to her like that. She wouldn't want it. Neither do I."

All of a sudden I feel like crying.

"So what do I do?" I ask my grandmother.

"Let someone in, Maxie. It don't have to be me or your daddy, but somebody."

I don't think I know exactly what she means, but then again, maybe I do, because now I can't stop crying. I know my grandma must be loving this, makes her feel like Oprah or something. She takes off her hat and puts it on the hook by the door.

"I thought you were going to church," I say, through my crying.

My grandma looks at me and smiles, which is a good thing because the thought of my grandma hating me is more than I can take.

"Baby, I just did," she says.

21

DRITA

"KOOL!" Maxie says when we are in the school library. On the table is a big round globe. I spin it around, looking for Kosova. This map is so old, it only shows one big country, Yugoslavia. It does not show how the world is today with the Balkans divided into many small countries. But this does not matter to me, I can still find my homeland easily.

"Here," I say, pointing to a small space near the center of Yugoslavia. On the map, my country is so small, it can fit underneath my finger. To me, it seems strange that such a little place has so many troubles.

On the other side of the world, Maxie touches New York City. It is a long way between our two fingers.

I think for a moment until I remember the right number that my father teaches me.

"*Tree thowzand kilometre,*" I say.

Maxie makes a whistle noise. The *bibliotekarja* looks at us.

"Quiet, girls!" she says. With her curly hair and round glasses, our librarian looks like a type of bird—the owl. Maxie must think so too, because now she whispers "whoo" like an owl and soon we are laughing so hard, we can't be quiet.

"Sssshhhh!" the library lady whispers, but I think she is only pretending to be angry, because now she is handing us another book, with many colorful pictures of kittens. Like me, Maxie likes animals, especially cats.

"Kool!" I say. Maxie smiles.

At first I thought Maxie and I are too different to be friends, but now I know in many ways we are the same. The biggest way is that Maxie likes things to be funny just like me.

Then the bell rings. Almost as soon as we begin to have fun together, lunch hour is over.

That night, when I am home with my family, I tell them about this.

"In my school, there is not so much time for friendships," I complain to my father as we finish dinner.

My grandmother puts some dishes in the sink. "That's all right," she says. "You need to concentrate on your lessons."

I do not understand why my grandmother says this. I thought she wanted me to make friends with Maxie.

But I am happy when my father agrees with me.

"Nonsense," he says. "This friend can probably teach Drita English faster than any school. It's only through conversation that one learns a new language."

I think about what happened in the library.

"Maxie did teach me some new words today. And we like to talk to each other very much," I tell him.

"See? Drita knows this already," he says to my grandmother.

From inside my mother's room, I can hear the television playing. Today, Nënë did not come out of her room even one time to talk to me. Maybe I can think of one thing that will cheer her up.

"Maybe I can invite Maxie over?" I ask.

"No," says Gjyshe.

"Yes," says my father.

"My son, are you forgetting something?" Gjyshe argues.

"Oh, Mother, Drita must enjoy her life too," he says.

"This is not the right time, Adem," my grandmother says, using my father's familiar name. But my grandmother knows she will have to agree with him. In Albania it is always like this: the father is in charge of the family.

"*Të shtunën* is the only day she should come. At least Miss Mirfue will be here to translate," my grandmother grumbles at last.

I am so happy, I climb on my father's lap and kiss him.

Then, with my father translating, I call Maxie's number and make the arrangements.

From the way she is putting the dishes in the sink, I know Gjyshe is upset, but when she sees how happy my friend will make everyone, I think she will change her mind.

I am so excited, I can't wait to tell my mother. When I finish on the telephone, I run into her room. She is asleep.

"My *shoge e ngushtë* is coming for a visit, Nënë! Isn't it wonderful?" I whisper.

My mother just shifts in the blanket and pulls her cover over her head.

Inside, I hope she is smiling.

22

Maxie

AFTER DRITA CALLS ME, I go straight into the kitchen.

"Who was that?" asks Grandma, drying off a plate.

"That girl Drita," I say, trying not to sound excited. "She invited me to her house."

Grandma doesn't say nothing, just reaches up into the cabinet and puts the plate on the rack.

"Well? Can I go?" I ask her even though I know I've got no chance. But Grandma surprises me.

"It's not up to me," she says.

"Who's it up to, then?" I ask.

Grandma looks at me like I'm the world's biggest dummy. "Who do you think?" she says.

I always thought that when my mother died, my grandma took over the job of being boss of the family. But sometimes, my daddy's more the boss than my grandma.

"Why don't you ask him?" she says, nodding her head toward the den. Suddenly, that door looks like the mouth of a lion's cave to me, and I don't want to go in case I get my head bit off. I pick up the dish towel from the edge of the sink.

"That's all right," I say, "I got chores to do."

Grandma takes the towel right back. "No, you don't," she says. "Go on in."

I sigh. My daddy's been so busy with his new job, it seemed like he was never going to get around to talking to me about that fight. Or that's what I was hoping, anyway.

I knock on my daddy's door, soft as a mouse. Maybe I'll be lucky and he'll be taking a nap or something.

"Yes?" my daddy growls. I can tell from the way he's got papers and things spread all over, he's been paying the bills.

"I need to talk to you," I say.

"So talk," he says without looking up.

"Drita invited me over to her house. I'm supposed to be writing my social studies report on her. For school."

"When?" my daddy says.

"On Saturday," I say.

"I see," he says, but the way he says it makes it sound like he doesn't see anything at all. Or even want to.

"Please, Daddy. It's for school."

"Drita was one of the girls involved in the fight, wasn't she?" my daddy says.

93

"Yes, but it wasn't her fault. Brandee was picking on her. She even hit her when she was down, Daddy."

"Your grandmother told me that part."

"See, Brandee wasn't playing fair. She broke the rules and then she was being a bully. Brandee was just mad because she couldn't show off."

"That didn't give you the right to hit her, Maxie."

I never understand why grown-ups always talk about "having the right" when they should be talking about "having the wrong." Everyone knows that slapping your former best friend upside her head is a bad idea.

"You think I don't know that?" I say.

"Frankly, Maxie, I don't know what's going on in your mind anymore."

It really makes me feel bad when my daddy says that. I can't help it when the waterworks start.

"I thought I was doing something nice for once, but instead all I did was make a big war between Drita and the rest of the girls in my class. I never even hit anyone before, least of all someone I once considered my friend. I think Brandee hates me now," I tell him, feeling about as bad as I can be.

"Come over here a second," Daddy says, kind of gruff.

"Why?"

"You got an eyelash."

In my family whenever you lose an eyelash, you get to

94

make a wish. I go over to him and my daddy takes it off my face.

"Make a wish," he says, and the next thing I know, my wish comes true 'cause I am sitting on his knee just like old times.

"Daddy. I don't fit no more," I tell him, but I'm just playing like I'm embarrassed.

"Yes, you do. And it's 'anymore,' not 'no more.' You know that. If there's one thing that gets on my nerves, it's hearing my daughter use slang," he says.

"Sorry, Daddy," I tell him. Out of his pocket he pulls a clean handkerchief so I can blow my nose.

"Now, tell me, if you were in the middle of this situation now—what could you do differently?" he asks, when I'm done.

"Nothing," I tell him.

"Think, Maxie," is all he says. So I do.

"Well. I guess I could have run and gotten a grown-up," I say after a minute. "I could have told them what Brandee was doing. But then Drita would have gotten beat up."

"It's possible."

"But that's not fair."

"No, it's not. That's true. But if you hit someone, that only make it worse."

"So, I should just stand by and watch it happen?"

"No. You've got to think of some other way to make Brandee stop."

"But that's impossible."

"Not impossible. Just hard."

"Okay, then. Very, very, very hard."

"Yes. It is very, very, very hard to walk away from a fight when you know you're right. But that's what you have to do."

"Why?"

"Because that's the only way to stop the fighting. Between two people or between two armies for that matter. One side has to stop and say 'we won't do this anymore.' "

"And let Drita get her butt kicked?"

"If that's what it takes. Because you know what? We've got laws for people who act like Brandee. What's the consequence in your school for hitting?"

"Losing your recess time for two weeks. Plus they call your house."

"Then that's the law. The law of the school yard. That's what civilization is all about."

It all seems so obvious, but at the same time, so big that I just sit there a moment on my daddy's lap, thinking about stuff. Finally, my daddy says:

"Now about Saturday . . ."

"Yeah?" I say, holding my breath.

"You can go," he says slowly, "but otherwise you're still

grounded. And your grandma has to come with you. Now you better go finish your homework. It's getting late."

I'm not about to argue with that. I put my hand on the doorknob. But then I remember something else I want to say.

"I'm sorry I was rude to your friend Lisa and her son," I tell him, and I mean it too. "If you like her, I guess she can't be that bad."

"She isn't that bad," he says. "I like her a lot. And I want you to try to like her too."

"Okay. I will. And I'm really sorry about her son too," I say. "I am really sorry for calling him a chump."

"That's all right. Everyone makes mistakes. Even my beautiful daughter," he says, grinning at me.

That's when I notice the T-shirt that he's got on, the one I gave him for Christmas last year.

"World's Best Dad" is written right across his chest. I think to myself, You can say that again.

23

DRITA

W HEN S ATURDAY COMES, I am so excited, I wake up too early, at 7:00. Today feels like a special day already because in the kitchen, there is my father, still eating his *mëngjez*. Usually my father goes to his taxi job when I am still sleeping.

"Are you ready for your visitor, Drita?" my father says. He is reading an Albanian newspaper, and drinking the thick, brown *kafe* my grandmother makes.

"Baba, I feel like it is *Ramazan*," I tell him. *Ramazan* is a holy time for Albanian people. When *Ramazan* is over, this is the best time for me because I always get too many presents.

"Silly girl. Eat your breakfast," my grandmother says. I do not know why she is so grumpy.

Miss Mirfue arrives just after my father leaves for work.

"*Zot!*" she says, coming into the kitchen. "There are too

many stairs in your building." Her breath is hard like some-one who is running too much.

"Do you have it?" says a voice. I turn around and there is my mother standing in the doorway. For the first time in many days, she is wearing regular clothes instead of just a dirty old nightgown.

"Good morning, Dashi, would you like some breakfast?" my grandmother says, as if there is nothing strange in this, but my mother doesn't answer her.

"Do you have it?" she asks again.

"Here, Dashi," Miss Mirfue says, holding out an enve-lope. *"Qofsh mirë!"* For good luck.

Every Saturday, Miss Mirfue comes to my house bringing many things for my family, like clothes and food. But today she is also bringing a special paper. It is a list with all the names of the Albanian people who have left Kosova and have reached safety in Macedonia. On this list, my mother hopes to find the name of Cousin Zana. Now my mother is taking this paper from Miss Mirfue.

"Kasamin, Kajim, Keku," she says, reading the names qui-etly. One hand is in her hair, and she is pulling on it.

"How is she?" Miss Mirfue says to my grandmother in a soft voice.

"See for yourself," says my grandmother. "No better. Worse, maybe."

For one moment, it is like something is happening to the air. I am dizzy in the head and my stomach is squeezing me hard. Now I know why my grandmother was upset with my friend coming. It is not because she did not want to know Maxie. It is because my mother is *çmendur*—not right in the head.

My grandmother was right and now it is too late and my friend is coming to visit.

Suddenly my mother starts to yell and cry.

"Thank God, thank God! Zana! Oh, Zana is safe!" she shouts, trembling all over.

We rush to her to see where my cousin's name is printed on the paper. This is happy news and good for us, but still my mother will not stop her crying.

"Please try to calm down, Nënë," I say and rub her arm.

"No, no, no!" my mother yells, falling against the table. Crash! Some plates fall on the floor. Pieces of them go everywhere.

My mother is lying on the floor, crying and crying. She won't get up.

Then I hear a terrible sound. The bell on the door is ringing again. My friend Maxie is right on time.

24

Maxie

"YOU SURE YOU WROTE THE RIGHT ADDRESS DOWN?" Grandma asks, leaning on the doorbell again.

"Yes, yes," I say, but now I'm not so sure. I swear, we've been standing there so long, we're just about to give up.

"Well, I guess we can always eat this pie ourselves," Grandma grumbles, picking up her shopping bag. My grandmother is the type of person that believes that when you visit someone, you should never go empty-handed, so she brought along a nice apple pie to give to Drita's family.

We're just about to go back down the stairs and get back in the car when suddenly, we hear the lock turning. Someone opens the door just a little tiny crack.

"*Chfa?*" a woman's voice goes from behind the chain.

"I'm Maxie and this is my grandma," I say. "I'm visiting Drita this afternoon."

At first when my father said Grandma had to come with me to Drita's house, I wasn't too excited about that, but now I'm glad she's here. The door closes again, and we hear a lot of noise and yelling in another language.

"What the heck is going on now?" Grandma mumbles, and I know she has to be pretty upset to say heck.

"Yes, hello?" says a middle-aged lady with a chubby face. The chain is off, but she only opens the door about an inch or two wider.

"Are you Mrs. Kelmendi?" Grandma asks.

"No. I'm a friend. Mrs. Kelmendi is resting."

From inside it sounds like anything but resting to me. In fact, it sounds more like a zoo with a lot of crying and screaming going on.

"Well, we were expected," says my grandmother to the half-closed door.

But finally, my friend Drita pops out.

"Maxie, come in!" she says and swings the door open wide.

Lying right in the middle of the kitchen floor is a lady. She's got light brown hair just like Drita, but instead of two neat braids, hers looks like a dirty cloud around her head. She's crying her eyes out, rocking all around like she's on one of those supermarket horses you got to put a quarter in to make it go. It looks like she's been throwing things too because all around her are a bunch of cups and broken dishes.

Over by the sink is a wrinkled-up old lady, who I bet is Drita's grandma. She's got a scared little baby pressed to her. He's crying too and she's talking to him real quiet like. If you ask me, she don't look too good herself.

"Mrs. Kelmendi is not well," says the chubby lady.

My grandmother steps over a broken plate and sets the pie down on the table. For a second nobody says anything. Then she rolls up her sleeves.

"What can we do to help?" she says.

25

DRITA

FOR ONE MOMENT, when the doorbell rings, I don't know what to do. My mother is lying on the floor like a little baby, crying and crying with broken plates everywhere. The doorbell keeps buzzing like an angry bee.

Outside the door, I hear Maxie's voice. She will go away if I don't answer.

She will go away.

For one moment, this thought pushes everything else out my head, even my grandmother, standing by the sink looking old and tired, even Miss Mirfue's frightened face, even my mother's tears. But then Miss Mirfue opens the door. I go with her.

Standing in the hall is my friend and a big woman. It must be Maxie's *gjyshe*, Mrs. Nichols. Mrs. Nichols is younger than my grandmother, and her skin is darker than Maxie's, but there is no surprise on her face when she walks into my house. Instead, she acts like it is a normal visit. She walks into the kitchen, picks up a plate off the floor and hands it to my grandmother.

"Thank you," Gjyshe says in English.

Miss Mirfue whispers something to Mrs. Nichols. Then Mrs. Nichols goes to my mother and says something to her in a quiet voice. She pats her head with her hand, calming her.

After a minute she turns to Maxie.

"Get the coats, Maxine," she says.

Down the stairs and out of the building we all go, and into a big blue car that smells like *vanilje*. Now Mrs. Nichols is driving us somewhere. All the while, Mrs. Nichols talks, talks, talks like there is nothing wrong or nothing strange about this. Mrs. Nichols even holds my mother's hand while she drives, like an old friend. Later on, I find out that for a long time this was Mrs. Nichols's job, to be a nurse at Roosevelt Hospital. Well, we are very lucky, I think, because she did a good thing for my family. She acted the right way not to scare my mother but to keep her peaceful.

Soon the car stops in front of a large white building. My heart starts to beat when I see the sign for the hospital, but as soon as we go inside, my fear goes away. The hospital is a big clean place with so many serious people. Two doctors come to talk to Nënë; one of them is quite pretty. They are talking to Miss Mirfue now, and Mrs. Nichols. Maxie and Hashim and I go into a special room they have for children there. It is like a playhouse with slides and toys and coloring books. Maxie is being very nice about everything that's happened. She even draws me a picture of a cat.

At last Miss Mirfue and Mrs. Nichols come into the room with us. In Albanian, Miss Mirfue tells me the hospital will take care of my mother for a few days. Hashim starts to cry, but I do not. For me this is good news. I think the Americans will take good care of my mother.

When we go home, we are all very tired and hungry too. My father is there waiting for us. I am surprised when I find out that my grandmother has called him from the hospital. My father even has a special dinner ready for us, a big paper bucket of chicken KFC. This food is very delicious to me, but even so, I am so tired, I can't finish. I put my head down on the table to rest. That is when I fall asleep.

Then I feel my father lifting me. It is a long time since my father carried me this way. He puts me in my bed while my grandmother tucks me in. It feels so good, I don't want to wake up.

"It's not good for the children to see their mother suffer so," my grandmother says.

"I suppose not," my father says.

"Don't worry, Adem," my grandmother says. "She will be home soon."

"I know," my father says. He puts his hand on my head and smoothes my hair.

"I think Drita chose the right friend," my *gjyshe* says.

"Yes, she did," Baba agrees and kisses me on the head. Softly, my father closes the door. In the darkness, I can see the picture Maxie drew for me, hanging by my bed. My *gjyshe* is right. Because of Maxie, now my mother will be better.

I hope so, anyway.

26

Maxie

WELL, DRIVING SOMEONE'S MOTHER to the hospital may not be the most normal thing to do the first time you get together with a friend, but that's exactly what happened. Me, Drita and her mother, the two grandmothers, Drita's baby brother and Miss Mirfue all piled into our SUV and drove on over to Roosevelt Hospital Emergency Room.

Those doctors took one look at Drita's mother and you could tell it's something serious because suddenly they're all over her and she's going down the hall in a wheelchair. Then me and Drita and her brother and my grandma spent a long time in this special room they got for kids there. I know my friend was pretty worried, but she seemed okay to me and wasn't crying or anything like I would be if it were my mom. And even though it wasn't exactly fun, we still had a pretty good time there drawing pictures and stuff like that.

Now today is Sunday and I wanted to go visit Drita's mom in the hospital as soon as I got up, but my grandma says no, not yet, she needs time to rest. She says we can visit her soon, and in the meantime she says maybe I can go shopping and buy Drita's mom a present. She says people need a lot of things when they go into the hospital and maybe we can think of something that will make her feel more comfortable.

"Maybe a nice housecoat," my grandma says.

"Grandma, you can't buy Drita's mom some funky old housecoat!"

"What's wrong with a good housecoat?" she asks. "I wear them all the time."

"Housecoats are okay if you're a grandmother. But Drita's mom is young," I say. "She's gotta have some style."

"You know, I think you're right, honey."

I have to say, I'm surprised that she's agreeing with me. Usually me and my grandma get in our biggest arguments about clothes.

"We need someone who's young and pretty and got some style to help us shop. Now who do we know like that?"

The way she asks that question, I can tell she's already got someone in mind.

27

DRITA

FOR THE FIRST TWO DAYS we are visiting her, my mother is only sleeping. Now today, on the third day when we come, I think she is asleep too, with her face turned to the wall.

My grandmother notices the empty food tray by the side of my mother's bed.

"It looks like your mother ate something! I will find the nurse and return the tray," she says as she leaves the room.

As soon as she's gone, my mother stirs in the bed.

"Oh," she says, opening her eyes. "Water."

My heart is beating so much. I run to the bathroom and fill her glass with water. When I come back, Nënë is sitting up in her bed.

"Here, Nënë," I say, handing her the glass. She drinks it right away.

My mother looks around. For a moment, she seems confused.

"Where is Baba? Where is the baby?" she asks.

"They are home."

"Home?"

"Yes, Nënë. You have been in the hospital two days already," I tell her.

"Two days? How is that possible?"

"You were sick, Nënë. We brought you here. Don't you remember?"

For a second, I am worried that maybe my mother doesn't remember things anymore. But then a look passes over her face and I know she does.

"Oh, yes. Of course."

Now my mother looks at me. "Drita, come here," she says. I go to my mother's bedside.

"Were you very frightened?" she asks.

"Yes, I was. I was afraid you were going to be sad forever."

My mother touches my head.

"*Zemra e nënës. Të keqen Nëna.*" she says. "Mommy's sweetheart."

"Are you sad now, Mother?" Because I see her tears.

"No, I am not sad. I am happy, because I am back with you, my love." More than anything, I hope my mother is right.

Just then Gjyshe comes hurrying back into the room.

"Ah, the sleeping beauty is awake," my grandmother says in a cheerful voice. She pulls back the curtains. Outside, the day is cool but sunny. In the light my mother's face seems younger. Not so tired.

"Did you show Nënë your pictures?" my grandmother says.

"What pictures, Drita?"

"I drew them for you in school. Do you want to see them?" I ask her.

"Very much," she says and opens the envelope I brought.

Already, I can tell my mother feels better because she studies the pictures carefully.

"Your drawing is very nice," she says finally, but then she points to one. "But who drew that?"

"My friend, Maxie."

"Oh, yes. One of your friends," my mother says. "The one who came to the house. I am so happy you are a popular girl, Drita."

Now my grandmother looks at me. Her eyes are asking a question: Well, Drita, will you tell the truth?

I want to tell her I am not really popular. But then I worry—what if I ruin everything. What if my mother cries again?

On the TV, I hear the happy music of a funny American

show with a big cartoon dog. In Kosova, my mother and I used to watch this show together, when I was little.

"Look, Nënë! Scooby!" I say. I am very glad that now there is something else to talk about.

"Oh, the silly dog! Turn on the sound, Drita!" she says, so I do. I climb into the bed with my mother and put my head on her shoulder.

Even though the story is too silly, we still like it. We start watching and before I know it, my mother is asleep again, her hair spread across the pillow like feathers.

I turn off the TV and sit there for a long time. I do not want to wake her, so I hardly breathe.

Sleep, Nënë, I think to myself. Get better soon.

28

Maxie

"How about this one?" Miss Thing—I mean, Lisa—says. She holds up a bathrobe.

"I don't think so," I say. "I'm not sure Drita's mom is a teddy bear person."

"You're right," she says. "Maybe teddy bears are a little too cute."

It's Sunday and me and my dad's girlfriend are shopping for Drita's mom at the Fulton Mall. It seems like we've gone into just about every store and we still haven't found anything that's right.

"Why don't you go look at those robes over there, while I check out the bargains," she says, spying another sales rack.

"Why do you always go there first, anyway?" I ask her.

In every store she's been like a hawk swooping down when she sees the word SALE.

Lisa smiles. "Honey, sales are my middle name," she says.

I walk over to a rack of shirts, start looking through them, but I don't see anything nice for Drita's mom.

"Oh my," goes Lisa. "My, my, my!" I look over to see what she found. It's a kimono-type robe with a little bit of silver sparkles on the sleeve. It's not just pretty. It's perfect.

"Is it a lot of money?" I say because it looks real expensive and I only got twenty dollars to spend on my present.

"It's not too bad. It's nineteen ninety-nine, plus there's thirty percent off," Lisa says.

"So how much would that be?" We just started to learn about percents in school and I'm not great at that yet.

"About fourteen dollars. We'll still be able to buy her those slippers you found before."

"Slippers?" I don't even remember any slippers.

"Don't you remember those cute little poofy purple things we saw when we came in? They were on sale too!" she says.

"Cool!" I say. I got to admit the woman does know a few things about shopping.

We go to stand on line so we can pay for the slippers and the robe. Then I figure it's time to take the subway home. It turns out I'm wrong about that.

"Come on," she says when we leave the store. "I want to take you to someplace else."

"Where are we going? Is it another sale?" I say, following her down the street. We stop at a store that's got a big sign that says KIDS SHOPPE.

"They got the cutest stuff in here," she says, opening the door. I look all around and see a little red shirt with sparkle letters on it. I look at the sleeve. Sixteen ninety-nine is what the tag says. It's exactly the kind of shirt I always want to buy, but my grandmother never lets me.

"I wish I had more money," I say because now I only have two dollars, forty-three cents left.

"Don't worry," she says. "This is on me."

I can hardly believe it. But then I hear my grandma's voice in my ears. "Don't take advantage" is what she would say.

"Isn't it kind of expensive?" I say in case she wants to change her mind.

"That's all right," she says. "A girl's got to have something special once in a while."

"Thanks!" I think I'm gonna look like a movie star in that shirt.

"You know, Maxie, I would never want to take her place."

"Who?" I ask because now I'm thinking about being a star one day.

"Your mama," she says.

"Oh," I say back.

"But I would like to be friends," Lisa says.

"That's fine with me," I say, because it is.

That Lisa gives me a big old smile.

Dimples! I think to myself. She sure is pretty.

"Now," she says, clapping her hands together. "How would you feel about a slice of Junior's cheesecake?"

29

DRITA

"YOO-HOO. ANYONE HOME?" says a voice. Maxie's grand-mother pushes the door open.

"Please, my friends, come in," my mother says from her bed.

Today my family and Miss Mirfue are all at the hospital for a special reason. Maxie and her grandmother are visiting my mother. It is the first time my friend will see her since she was sick.

For one moment, Maxie stands at the door like she doesn't know what to do.

But then my father jumps up.

"How do you do?" he says in English and shakes Maxie's hand. Because my father was working when Nënë got sick, he never got to meet Maxie and her grandmother, but I can tell from Baba's face he likes them right away.

"Hello," Miss Mirfue says to Mrs. Nichols. "So nice to see you again." My father arranged for Miss Mirfue to be here too, in case we needed a translator.

"Hello, Maxie," I say, even though we are just seeing each other in school only a few hours ago.

"Hey, Drita," she says back. Then my brother runs over.

"Hellohellohello!" he says. Everyone laughs to hear my brother speak English, but my friend's face stays serious.

"Maxie has something for you!" says Mrs. Nichols. Maxie takes a box out of the big bag she is holding. She gives it to my mother.

"I hope you get well soon," says Maxie.

Very carefully, my mother unties the box.

"Lovely," my mother says when she sees what is inside. Her smile is so big. Now I remember what a beautiful woman Nënë is, with her long brown hair and pretty smile.

Baba must think so too. "Dashi, you look like a queen!" he says when Nënë puts on the blue robe.

"Thank you!" my mother says to my friend.

"You're welcome," Maxie says and then she stands there like she does not know what to do. My mother jumps from the bed and gives her a big hug.

"Sweet girl!" Nënë says in Albanian.

Maxie hugs her back.

Then I remember that my family has a big surprise too. I go over to Miss Mirfue.

119

"Miss Mirfue," I say to her, "tell Maxie and her grandmother our good news."

"Zot, Drita, tell them yourself! Your English is good enough," she says. I know she is right.

So then I tell Mrs. Nichols myself. "Mrs. Nichols, tomorrow Mother goes home."

"Congratulations!" Mrs. Nichols says, and she kisses my head.

Soon everyone is talking in Albanian and English. I think my friend Maxie will be happy too. But when I look at her, I realize she is not even listening. She is just standing by the door, and her eyes are watching my mother.

"Come on, baby girl," Maxie's *gjyshe* says softly, putting her arm around Maxie's shoulder. "Time to go."

Maxie puts her face against her grandmother. I feel so strange because now I see my friend is unhappy.

"Did I say something wrong?" I ask Gjyshe when they leave. "Why didn't they stay?"

My grandmother looks at my mother and my mother looks at me.

"Kush e di si e ka hallin," she says in Albanian. Sometimes there is more to people than meets the eye.

30

Maxie

TUESDAY AFTERNOON ALWAYS MEANS THE SAME THING in my class: project time. When we were studying colonial times, I thought project time was kind of boring. But now, I like project time much more because Drita is my partner.

"You seen the glue sticks?" yells a boy. It's Samuel. He and Jordan are partners, and they're making a map of ancient Egypt.

"No, I haven't seen no glue sticks," I say back. Now can you please keep it quiet?

"Guys. We need to keep our voices down," Miss Salvato says because the only problem with project time is my class sometimes gets noisy. Then she comes over to us.

"How's the project going?" Miss Salvato says, looking over the map that me and Drita are making.

"Good," says Drita, carefully. Her English is getting better every day, especially now that she's got me helping her.

"I like how you drew the map key, Maxie," says Miss Salvato.

"Actually, that was Drita's idea," I tell her.

"I was wondering if the two of you would like to work in the hallway," says Miss Salvato. I look over at Drita to see if she understands, and she just nods.

"Yes, please," I say. Because it's kind of a privilege in my class when you get to work by yourself in the hallway.

"C'mon, Drita," I say, and we pick up our stuff and go out into the hall. But when we go out there, it turns out we're not alone after all, because someone else is out there too, sitting on the floor reading her book.

"Brandee's working in the hall too," Miss S. says. "But I'm sure you won't bother each other."

"Hi, Brandee," I say. Drita and I put our map stuff down on the floor. But Brandee just sniffs and looks the other way.

Even though I wrote her a letter saying I was sorry like I was supposed to, now homegirl won't even talk to me. She even acts like I'm invisible. And since we're still in the same class together, that's pretty hard to do.

"Okay, whatever. Don't talk to me, see if I care," I say. After all, it's not like me and Drita don't have a lot of work to do. This week, we've got to finish our whole map and then write a report. So we just get busy. After a while, I realize Brandee is standing right there, watching us.

"You making a map or something?" she says.

"Yeah. It's Kosovo," I say.

"That's her place, right?" Brandee asks.

"Yes, this is my country. Only, my people call it Kosova," Drita says, holding out a Magic Marker. "You want to help?"

"No!" Brandee says, and then she picks up all her stuff and moves down the hall like we got the chicken pox or something.

Drita just looks at me and shrugs. I guess Brandee's probably never gonna like Drita, but that don't even matter. Suddenly I get this idea.

"Hey, Drita, now that your mother's feeling better, would you like to come to my house for a sleepover?"

Drita just looks at me, and I can tell she doesn't get what I'm asking her.

That's all right. I'm sure I can make her understand.

31

DRITA

"DRITA, HOLD STILL," my mother says, smiling at me.

"Ow," I say, because now the comb she is holding has hit a knot, pulling my hair. In Albania, one of my mother's jobs was as a hairdresser. Now that she is feeling better, she begins to practice for her old job again. One bad part of this—too many hairstyles for me!

But then my mother is finished.

"Gorgeous!" my mother says in English, looking at me.

One thing that surprises me very much, when my mother comes back from the hospital, is how much she likes to speak English. She practices every day. My mother is a fast learner. Already she knows as much as me and sometimes even more.

I look at myself in the mirror. My mother has made me look like a queen.

"Such a pretty girl. No wonder all the Americans love you," she says with a smile.

An uncomfortable feeling comes inside me. I put down the mirror.

"What's wrong, *e bukura e mamit?*" my mother asks. For a long time, I can't think of the words I want to tell her, but then I do.

"Nënë," I say, finally. "I am not *kam shoge shumë*—very popular. I didn't tell you because I didn't want you to worry. I don't have so many friends. The other girls at my school, they don't like me too much. Maxie is the only one."

Even though I know my mother is much, much better, and will not cry when I tell her this, I still feel worried to upset her. But now I am surprised when I see the smile on her face.

"That's okay," she says.

"You mean you knew?" I say. My mother bends down and she is kissing me.

"Drita, don't you know? It's better to have one true friend than to have a million others," she says. "I am glad you have found a *shoge të ngushte.* When I look at Maxie, I know she is a good girl. I think she will be your friend for a long time."

When my mother looks at me, I notice once again how round and brown her eyes are. To me they are as warm as the sun.

Beep, goes a car horn on the street. It's my friend's big blue car waiting to take me to her house. I hug my mother as tight as I can.

"Have fun, my girl. Don't stay up too late," she says.

"And don't forget the *byrek me qumësht!*" Gjyshe shouts from the kitchen. Now my grandmother comes into the room holding something. It is a special present she has made for Maxie's family to thank them for their kindness. When I pick up the *byrek* she has baked, the plate still feels warm in my hand.

I quickly kiss her good-bye.

"*Mirë upafshim,*" Gjyshe says as I run out. "See you to-morrow!"

"What took so long?" Maxie says when I climb in the door. In the front seat, Maxie's grandmother Mrs. Nichols is smiling at me.

"Hello, Mrs. Nichols, how are you today?" I say carefully.

"I'm good. And I swear, Drita, your English gets better every time I see you."

This is such a good compliment for me, I feel my face getting red. "Thank you!" I say.

Then I remember something. "From my family, to say thank you very much." I hand her the dish.

"You're welcome very much!" says Mrs. Nichols. "That sure smells good."

At Maxie's house there is very much to do, because now

I am helping her with a big *projekt* she is writing for school. On her computer Maxie has written down many facts about my country, and about me too, because the subject of her report is my journey to America. At first when I found this out, I was embarrassed, but now I am glad to help her by answering more questions, and drawing a map.

We are working all the way through dinner and at night too. Finally at ten o'clock, Maxie's grandmother claps her hands.

"Time for bed, girls!" she says.

As a present, my father bought me some new pajamas. Now I don't have to wear my old torn kind with the feet.

"Cool pajamas," Maxie says when I come out of the bathroom.

"I made you a bed in Maxie's room," Mrs. Nichols says, opening the door to Maxie's room.

I think my friend is so lucky. Her room is very nice. Her bed is purple with toy animals on it. On her wall, she has many posters of animals, especially cats, which I like too. Next to the window, there is a home for an animal. When I tap on the side, a fat little hamster comes over to kiss my finger.

"Her name is Cupcake," Maxie says.

Then I see something else. On one table there are some things. I go over to look.

This is what I see: a gold ring, and a lady's watch, also gold. A pretty bottle and pictures in frames. I pick one up. Inside, it shows a beautiful lady holding a baby. I look at my friend, where she is sitting on the bed. Now I think I understand something.

"Your mother, she is *vdekur*?" I say, forgetting that my friend does not speak Albanian.

But I think she understands anyway. Maxie puts her head down.

Now I know the secret of my friend. It is not a secret about boys or friends or superstars. It is not the kind of secret two children might tell each other on a funny American TV show. It is a real secret, and something close to her heart. And now, I am very glad to share it.

I do not know the right words in English for when I put my arm around her shoulder.

"*Më vjen shumë keq,* Maxie," is all I can say. I am so sorry.

32

Maxie and DRITA

"MAXIE! DRITA! Help me move this table!" my teacher says, grabbing one end of the long worktable we got in our classroom.

"Where does this go?" I ask. Miss S. points over to the wall.

"I just want to move it back a couple of feet. That way the families will have room to walk around all the dioramas. . . ."

"Watch out!" says Brandee because Drita almost bumps into her. When she realizes we're just helping out, she sniffs and keeps working on her report about the French Revolution. If you ask me, dressing a Barbie doll up like Marie Antoinette is pretty dumb, but my teacher said it showed imagination.

Today is a big day for our class. It's Project Day, which

means that all of the kids in our class get to invite their families to a big celebration so that we can share our social studies projects with them. Right now, a whole bunch of parents are waiting in the hall for us to finish setting up.

"Are you nervous?" I ask Drita.

Drita shakes her head no. When she does, a whole bunch of little braids bounce around her head. That's one thing that really surprised me when she came to school this morning—Drita in cornrows.

"What about you, Maxie, are *you* nervous?" Drita asks.

"Kind of," I tell her. But that's not really true unless "kind of" means "kind of a lot."

"Don't worry, Maxie, I think you will do a great job," she says and gives me a pat on the back.

See, the reason I got so much pressure on me is because I'm the one person in my class who has to read their report in front of everyone. My dad says it's an honor, but I don't know about that. I don't have the time to feel nervous, though, because now my teacher opens the door. All kinds of people come streaming into the room.

"Welcome to Project Day," my teacher says.

It seems like everyone and his brother is walking around our classroom oohing and ahhing at all the projects. There's Jordania's mom and dad looking at the Roman Coliseum she made out of modeling clay. They're the tallest people in the room, just like their daughter. There's Brandee's mom, all dressed up and fancy-looking, fussing over her Barbie Antoinette. And there's Mr. Littman standing in line to see Kayla's diorama of King Tut's tomb.

The room is crowded with people, but neither me or Drita have seen our families yet. Then I look over at the door.

"It looks like the Maxie and Drita bus just arrived," I say because now my grandma and daddy, and Drita's mom, dad, grandma and baby brother all come walking into the room at once. There are lots of kisses and hellos going all around.

"I like your hair!" my grandma says to Drita.

"Nënë did it!" Drita says, shaking her head so her braids bob up and down.

"Mrs. Kelmendi, maybe one day you can do my hair too!" I say.

"Maxie, of course!" Mrs. Kelmendi says. "Now please come here."

"What for?" I ask.

"I want to fix shirt." I go over to her so she can straighten out my collar. "There. You look so nice. Are you ready?" she asks.

"Oh, she's ready," my grandmother says.

"Now don't be nervous!" my daddy says.

Over his shoulder, I see someone walk into the classroom.

"Don't turn around," I tell him. Because I want it to be a surprise. Miss Surprise comes up and taps him on the shoulder.

"What are you doing here?" Daddy says when he sees who it is.

"Maxie invited me," Lisa says. "She called me on my cell phone first thing this morning. Hi, girlfriend," she says and gives me a peck on the cheek.

"Hi," I say back.

My dad looks so shocked, I swear his chin almost hits the floor.

At the front of the room, Miss Salvato raises her voice so that everyone can hear. "Kids, friends and family members. If you'll take a seat, we'll get started."

Everyone sits down in the folding chairs we set up at the front of the room. There are so many people, a few of the kids have to sit on the windowsill, but no one minds. Now my teacher nods her head at me.

"Okay, Maxie," she says, "you're on."

I feel so nervous, for a second I think I'm going to faint, but I don't.

"Yo Maxine!" someone yells, sassing me.

"Don't you razz me, Jordan," I yell back, "I know where you live." And the whole room laughs, 'cause I guess this has got to be my funniest joke ever.

I take a deep breath just like my grandmother told me. The room quiets down. Then I start.

"On October fifteenth, current events came to our school. And I don't mean current events in the way we usually get them here, which is kind of boring, but I mean news, real news.

"I don't know if you know about Kosova. I didn't. I mean, I might have heard the words on the television, and seen the pictures, but they didn't mean a thing to me until I met a girl named Drita. Then I started to find out more.

"Kosova is in the Balkans. It's very pretty and there are a lot of trees and mountains. But there's a war there between the Serbians and the Kosovars and it's been going on a long time. No one knows who started it, and no one knows how it will end, but there are a lot of Kosovars killed or missing, just because of who they are. A lot of people are afraid and are running away, even mothers with little babies. Someone who runs away from a war is called a refugee and that's who Drita's people are. Refugees. Runaways.

"The way Drita tells it, Kosova was a good place to live once. There were fun places to go like the park or the market, and they did stuff like watch soccer games. Her family, the Kelmendis, felt safe. But then something started to change.

"Some days, kids would throw rocks at her on the way to

school. Other days she would hear gunshots. Then some people got taken away in the middle of the night. Drita's mom looked everywhere for her favorite cousin, but no one knew where she went to. Soon her family got too afraid to go outside. Her daddy had already left to come here, and he was supposed to send for them. But they didn't hear from him for a long time, because in the war all the phones stopped working.

"Then one night her grandmother shook her. She didn't even have time to pack, but that was all right because Drita's family slept in their clothes, waiting. Her mother carried her down the street, where there was a bus. It was full of people and lots of kids, all scared, all wanting to leave.

"They drove a long time, she says, and she was scared the whole way but never cried, not even when some soldiers on the border of a country called Macedonia stopped the bus. Everyone was afraid the soldiers would keep them, but they didn't, they let them go.

"Ten days later, Drita was here, in New York. It was the first time she had seen her daddy in over a year, but her family was lucky. Not only did they get out, but her father had a job and an apartment all ready for them.

"But when I met her, I didn't know about Drita's story. All I knew is she was a new girl, and different from me. That made it easy for me to laugh at her in the beginning. But then when I got to know Drita, I started finding out that even though on the outside we were different, on the inside we were just the same. I'm real lucky I got to know her because she's a really great person and a good friend. But you don't have to take my word for it. You can find out about her yourself."

Just like we planned it, Drita jumps out of her seat and comes running over.

"Now," I say to everyone, "who has a question for Drita, my homegirl?"

I don't even believe it! It seems like every person in the room raises their hand at once.

"Maxie, who should I call on first?" Homey says, looking out over the sea of hands.

"I don't know, Drita, but something tells me you're about to have a lot of new friends."